JF NIGHT
Night, P. J., author.
You can't come in here!

W9-BEU-839

You're invited to a

CREEPOVER ®

You Can't Come in Here!

Fountaindale Public Library
Bolingbrook, IL
(630) 759-2102

written by P. J. Night

SIMON SPOTLIGHT
New York   London   Toronto   Sydney   New Delhi

This book is a work of fiction. Any references to historical events, real people, or real places are used fictitiously. Other names, characters, places, and events are products of the author's imagination, and any resemblance to actual events or places or persons, living or dead, is entirely coincidental.

SIMON SPOTLIGHT
An imprint of Simon & Schuster Children's Publishing Division
1230 Avenue of the Americas, New York, New York 10020
This Simon Spotlight hardcover edition July 2018

Copyright © 2011 by Simon & Schuster, Inc. All rights reserved, including the right of reproduction in whole or in part in any form.
SIMON SPOTLIGHT and colophon are registered trademarks of Simon & Schuster, Inc.
YOU'RE INVITED TO A CREEPOVER is a registered trademark of Simon & Schuster, Inc.
Text by Michael Teitelbaum
For information about special discounts for bulk purchases, please contact Simon & Schuster Special Sales at 1-866-506-1949 or business@simonandschuster.com.
Designed by Nick Sciacca
Manufactured in the United States of America 0618 FFG
10 9 8 7 6 5 4 3 2 1
ISBN 978-1-5344-1658-1 (hc)
ISBN 978-1-4424-2095-3 (pbk)
ISBN 978-1-4424-2157-8 (eBook)
Library of Congress Catalog Card Number 201047765

CHAPTER 1

The tall, black-clad man stepped slowly toward the sleeping woman who was stretched out on the couch. Behind him, pale light from a mist-shrouded moon trickled in through a broken window. In the distance, the mournful wail of a wolf split the deathly still night. The man strode one step closer, brushing past a spiderweb, sending the eight-legged creature scurrying up its silvery strands. Reaching the couch, the man parted his brilliant red lips, revealing two long, sharp, gleaming white fangs.

"And now, my dear," the man said softly, leaning down toward the woman's exposed throat, "you will be mine—forever!"

As the man's fangs closed in on her neck, the woman suddenly awoke. Her eyes shot open in horror as she stared up at the beastlike jaws moving quickly toward her.

"AAAIIIEEEEEE!" she screamed, but her cry went unanswered.

Almost.

"Emily? Is that you? Is everything all right? I heard a scream," said a voice drifting down the basement stairs. Downstairs, in her family's home theater, Emily Hunter hit the pause button on the DVD's remote.

"Yeah, Mom, I'm fine," Emily replied, shaking her head. *Why does she always interrupt me just at the good part?* she wondered, staring at the horrific image frozen on the big screen in front of her.

"Well, I'm home, honey," Emily's mom called down. "You watching a scary movie again?"

"Yeah, Mom. I like scary movies, remember?" Emily shouted up the stairs.

"Okay, dinner will be ready in about half an hour," her mom replied. "Dad will be home any minute."

Emily glanced at the clock. It read 8:10. She shook her head.

"I bet I'm the only kid in the entire country who eats dinner at eight thirty," Emily mumbled to herself. Then she shrugged and hit play.

Up on the screen, the man had the woman locked in his supernatural gaze. She was spellbound by his stare, unable to move, trapped by his dark, penetrating eyes. He bit down hard, sinking his teeth deeply into her neck. She went limp in his arms, not dead, but no longer truly alive. The vampire's victim had been ushered into the world of the undead.

"Cool!" Emily said. Then she hit rewind and watched the scene again.

"Hey, Em, I'm home!" came her dad's voice from the top of the stairs.

"Hi, Dad," Emily shouted up to him, pausing the movie again.

"How was your day?" her dad asked.

"Good, thanks."

"Great," her dad said. "I'll see you in a few for dinner."

As she went back to the movie, Emily thought about the long hours that both her parents worked. Her mom was a lawyer. Her dad, a vice president of a pharmaceutical company. Emily knew that without all their hard work she would not be sitting in a state-of-the-art home theater watching one of her favorite horror movies. And if letting herself in after school, spending a few hours alone, and eating dinner at eight thirty instead of six like the rest of the world was the price, well, she figured she didn't have it all that bad.

As the undead man and woman on the screen stepped from the old gothic mansion in search of fresh victims, the credits rolled, and Emily's mom called her for dinner.

"On my way, Mom!" she shouted, flipping off the TV and bounding up the stairs.

"So what did you do at school today?" her dad asked as he passed Emily a bowl of mashed potatoes.

"Nothing too exciting," Emily replied, scooping potatoes onto her plate next to a mound of string beans. "I had to climb the rope in gym. You know how much I love that. But chem lab was fun. Ethan and Hannah were lab partners. And Ethan put too much red powder in with the blue powder, and white smoke and bubbles started pouring out of the beaker, all over the lab table and the floor. It was so funny!"

"I always said Ethan was a born scientist," her father teased. "Hey! How about we play some Wii after dinner?"

"Can't," Emily replied through a mouthful of string beans. "Going across the street to hang out at Drew and Vicky's."

"So late?" her mom asked. "We're getting up early tomorrow to drive to the beach."

"It's Friday night, Mom. And besides, I'll be home by my nine thirty curfew and I'll go straight to bed," Emily said. "I promise."

"It seems like you're always going over there," her mom said, shaking her head. "Are you embarrassed by your own house?"

"Of course not. Drew and Vicky just feel more comfortable at their own house, I guess."

"I don't know how anyone could feel comfortable in that house," her mom said. "It's a wreck."

"That house has been a wreck for all the years we've lived here," Emily pointed out. "That's not their fault."

"Yes, but it was empty for a long time," her mom said. "When I heard that someone had bought it and was moving in, I was thrilled. I figured they'd fix it up. But the Strigs have been there for a few months now, and they haven't done a thing. The siding is still ripped up. The old shutters hang from the windows. The porch is about to collapse, and the next big storm we get will probably take that roof down. The lawn is brown and dead. They haven't planted a single flower. It's just a disgrace to this neighborhood. Your father and I and the rest of the people on this street work hard to have a nice place to live, and a nice community."

Emily looked away for a second, then she turned back to her mother. "I just think you don't like Drew and Vicky," she said. "But you only met them once for, like, two minutes. You don't even know them."

"Oh, honey, it's not true that I don't like Drew and Vicky," Mrs. Hunter explained. "But it is true that I've never even *seen*, much less *met*, their parents. Normally I'd insist on meeting them before you hung out at their house, but I guess it's okay since you're only right across the street."

"You know that there aren't any other kids in the neighborhood, Mom," Emily said. "Everyone's old, even older than you and Dad, and now I finally have some kids my own age around here. They're a lot of fun to hang out with and I just want to be friends with them. So what if I go over to their house all the time?"

Emily's mom sighed. "All right, go have fun," she said, knowing how much Emily missed having other kids around. Then she scowled slightly. "But I still wish their parents would fix up that house."

"I'll tell them that, Mom," Emily joked, getting up

from the table and bringing her plate into the kitchen. Then she kissed her mom and hurried across the dining room. "Bye. See ya later."

Emily bolted out the front door before her mom could say anything more. She glanced up and down the block. House after house looked pretty much the same. The soft glow of streetlights and porch lights revealed muted-color siding, sliding glass doors leading onto decks, nicely mowed lawns, landscaped gardens, and blacktop driveways.

And then there was the Strig house.

Looking across the street, Emily saw the ramshackle old place. The last few flakes of paint on the original wooden clapboard danced in the wind. The sun-bleached shutters dangled on rusty nails. Most of the windows were broken, and those that weren't were boarded up. Green moss spread across the roof. The front lawn had died long ago, and even the weeds seemed to be struggling to survive.

Emily realized that her mom was right. The place looked as if no one had lived there for years. But she knew better. She knew that a family with two kids was living there. And they liked her. They wanted to hang out with her, and she liked hanging out with them. They had a lot of cool stuff in their house. And that was good enough for Emily.

She walked across the crunchy brown lawn and stepped up onto the porch. Ancient floorboards creaked as she approached the front door. Emily was about to knock when she felt a tap on her shoulder. She jumped at the touch, spun around, and found herself face-to-face with Drew Strig.

Drew was taller than Emily, and very thin. His face was pale. His jet-black hair sprang out in every direction and looked as if it hadn't had even a chance meeting with a hairbrush in years. His black T-shirt and jeans looked slightly too small for his body.

"You scared me!" Emily exclaimed, and started to laugh. "I didn't hear you step onto the porch."

"Sorry about that," Drew said. "I wasn't sure you were going to make it over tonight."

"Yeah, my mom gave me a hard time," Emily explained. "You know, the usual. 'It's so late. Why are you always going over there?'"

"Maybe she doesn't like us," said a voice from above.

Looking up, Emily spotted Drew's sister, Vicky, sitting on a branch in an old gnarled tree that spread out across the front yard and overhung the tattered porch. Vicky looked very different from her brother. Her hair was pure white, but not old-lady white, more like glowing platinum. It hung down to her shoulders in perfectly straight strands extending from the part in the middle of her head. There was never a strand out of place. Her skin was the same color as her hair, and her thin lips had an odd purplish tint to them.

She was as skinny as her brother and almost as tall. Her black oversize shirt extended below her waist. The sleeves were so long, they hid her hands. Her clothes were dirty, but she didn't smell bad. She smelled kind of sweet and earthy, like the way the dirt smelled when Emily's mom churned up the garden each spring. To Emily, Vicky looked like some kind of goth-hippie hybrid. In fact, Emily thought that both Drew and Vicky dressed like rock stars. Emily, with her long, curly, reddish brown hair, sneakers instead of boots, and often sunburned face (from always forgetting to put on sunscreen before she went outside), never thought she looked as cool as these two.

"Nah," Emily responded. "It's not that she doesn't like you guys. I think she just doesn't like your house."

Vicky nodded and pushed herself off the branch. She dropped down onto the porch without making a sound and without the slightest stumble.

"Nice move," Emily said. "You should try out for the school gymnastics team."

"But I don't go to your school," Vicky said, lifting herself onto the porch railing, which shifted slightly even under her light weight.

"You could probably still join the team though," said Emily. "It's a bummer you guys are homeschooled. Any chance that'll change next year?"

"Not likely," Drew answered. "Our parents would just rather have us stay home and teach us themselves."

Emily shrugged.

"Your parents around tonight?" she asked, glancing up at the house and noticing that every window was dark.

"Yeah," Drew said. "Somewhere in the house."

Emily nodded as Vicky slipped off the railing and walked past her without making a sound. She followed, noticing that the floorboards creaked loudly beneath her own clumsy feet.

Drew pushed open the front door. It swung inward

with a woeful squeak. Emily followed Drew and Vicky inside.

"Drew, Vicky? Is that you?" called out a woman's voice.

"We're upstairs," added a man's voice.

"Ah, Mom and Dad," Drew said to Emily. "Told you they were around here somewhere." Then he cupped his hands around his mouth and shouted, "Yeah, it's us, Mom! Emily's here. She's gonna hang out for a while."

"Hi, Mr. and Mrs. Strig," Emily called up as she closed the front door.

Emily followed Drew and Vicky deeper into the house. This was not the first time she had been inside, but the weird layout of the place always surprised her a bit. It was so different from her own house right across the street. Just inside the front door, there were two narrow hallways, formed by unpainted Sheetrock walls. One turned to the left. The other led to a large room that was made entirely of wood paneling. And not just the walls, but the floor and ceiling too, as if someone had found a bunch of the stuff on sale and decided to build a whole room out of it.

"Ah, the famous Strig rec room," Emily said as they stepped in.

"We like it," Vicky said, somewhat defensively.

"Hey, I like it too," Emily replied quickly. "Who wouldn't?"

The room looked as if it had been magically transported here from a college dormitory. Its main furnishings were a Ping-Pong table and a foosball table, plus a couple of ripped-up chairs and a table with an old-fashioned rotary dial phone. A line of electric guitars and amplifiers stood in a row along one wall. A stereo, complete with a record turntable, sat in one corner. Next to it stood stacks and stacks of vinyl LPs. Drew turned on the stereo and put an album on the turntable. Punk music filled the room.

"Don't your parents mind you playing music so loud?" Emily shouted as she flipped through the stack of albums.

"Nah," Drew replied. "Whose records do you think these are?"

"Ready to lose?" Vicky asked, stepping up to the foosball table and grabbing the handles on one side. Emily took the other side and spun her players a few times.

"Game on," she said, dropping the ball onto the table.

Emily and Vicky slammed and twisted the game's

handles, making the little plastic players they controlled kick the ball. Vicky reacted instinctively when Emily fired a shot at her goal. Her goalie blocked the shot, then she deftly passed the ball through Emily's defense and fired it into the goal.

"Ugh," Emily moaned, spinning a handle in frustration. "How are you so good at this game?"

Vicky smiled at her friend. "I've had a lot of practice. Don't worry, once you've played as much foosball as I have, you'll beat me. Another game?"

Emily sighed. It was nice that Vicky tried to make her feel better, but she knew that she could practice all day and all night for weeks and she'd never be as good as Vicky. "Sure, why not."

As Emily and Vicky played another game, Drew chose the music, playing a song or two from one album, then another. When Vicky had beaten Emily two more times, Drew turned off the stereo and picked up a guitar.

"Wanna play some tunes?" he asked Emily, gesturing to another guitar.

"Or I could just beat you at Ping-Pong now," Vicky added.

Tough choice. Emily's dad had taught her to play a

little guitar, but she didn't practice as often as she would have liked, since it was kind of boring playing alone. She loved playing guitar with Drew and Vicky, who had been playing for far longer than she had. She always had a great time with them, and she could feel her playing improve. On the other hand, she'd love nothing more than to pay Vicky back by thrashing her at Ping-Pong.

But before Emily could decide, her cell phone sounded with a text message alert. Pulling out her phone, she saw that the message was from her mother. It simply said, IT'S NINE THIRTY.

"Ah, my mother, the human alarm clock," Emily said. "Sorry, guys, I promised her I'd be home by nine thirty."

"See you tomorrow night?" Drew asked.

"Can't," Emily said. "My parents have the whole weekend planned. We're spending all of Saturday and Sunday at the beach. Kind of a 'summer's almost here' thing."

"Bummer," Vicky said. "But we'll see you Monday?"

"Definitely! See you later."

Emily hurried across the street and slipped into her house. Her mother and father were in the living room watching TV. Franklin, their black cat, was curled up on her father's lap.

"I'm here!" Emily announced. "Nine thirty-two on the dot. Just like we agreed."

"Cute," her mom said. "Thanks for coming home right away. Did you have fun? What did you do?"

"Played games and stuff, you know," Emily replied.

"Video games?" her mom asked.

"No, they don't have a TV, actually," Emily said. "We played foosball."

"Foosball?" her dad said. "I played that all the time in college. Great game. I am definitely a master. Maybe I could join you some time?"

"Dad!" Emily groaned.

"Just kidding," her dad said.

"All right, hon," her mother said. "Time for you to get some sleep. I'm going to wake you at seven tomorrow morning."

Emily grimaced. Waking up early was not her thing. "Really? That early?"

"The early bird doesn't get stuck in traffic," her father reminded her.

Emily smiled as she trotted up the stairs to her room. That was one of her dad's signature corny phrases.

After brushing her teeth and changing into her

pajamas, Emily flopped onto her bed, popped in her earbuds, and turned on her iPod. She imagined playing the guitar chords herself. It wasn't long before she got sleepy and took out her earbuds. Emily snuggled under the covers.

A-hooooo! Ow-ow-w! came a loud, gut-piercing howl. Emily felt the blood freeze in her veins, then remembered the DVD she had been watching. *Dad must have turned on that movie. Jeez, he scared me half to—*

A-HOOOOO! OW-OW-W!

This time the howl was louder, and Emily knew instantly that it wasn't coming from the basement and it was too loud to be coming from the TV. The bone-chilling shriek was coming from outside.

She dashed across her room, stumbling over a stack of books she had left on the floor. Catching herself on her windowsill, she peered out the window. There, on the Strigs' brown front lawn, a huge wolf loped toward the house. It had to be bigger than a car. The wolf's back legs were long and slender, its chest round and muscular. Matted gray fur extended down its powerful front legs in mud-stained clumps.

But it was when Emily caught sight of the wolf's jaws

16

that her heart rose into her throat. Was that blood on the animal's long snout? The wolf opened its mouth wide and howled again, revealing long white fangs flecked with specks of red.

A little yelp escaped from Emily's throat as porch lights up and down the block flicked on. Seeming to sense her watching it, the wolf glanced over its shoulder, then quickly turned back toward the Strigs' front door. Crouching low, as if it were stalking prey, the wolf slowly climbed the stairs onto the front porch.

"Drew and Vicky," Emily muttered in horror. "It's gonna hurt Drew and Vicky!"

She turned and dashed from her room. Practically flying down the stairs, she exploded out the front door. Running across the street, she felt her heart pound as she watched the wolf lunge toward the door.

"Get away from there!" Emily shouted.

At the sound of her voice, the wolf turned and stared right at her, baring its razorlike teeth and growling. Then the snarling beast turned back, pushed the door open with its snout, and walked right into the house.

"No!" Emily cried, running faster now. Reaching the porch, she took the stairs two at a time, then stopped short at the front door. She pushed the door open slowly, straining to see inside without actually sticking her head through the doorway. Pushing back against the terror shooting through her body, and shoving aside all thoughts of her own safety, Emily burst into the Strigs' house.

CHAPTER 2

"Drew, Vicky? Is that you?" Mrs. Strig called out from upstairs as Emily stepped through the doorway.

"We're upstairs!" Mr. Strig shouted.

"Mr. Strig! Mrs. Strig! You've got to get out of here!" Emily cried. "There's a wolf in your house!"

She got no reply.

Oh no! Emily thought in horror. *I hope the wolf hasn't gone upstairs and cornered them! Where are Drew and Vicky?*

Emily crept slowly toward the rec room. As she walked, she strained to hear any sound coming from the end of the hall.

She heard nothing.

She also felt the rush of courage she had experienced wearing off—quickly.

What am I doing? she wondered, inching closer to the rec room. *What can I possibly do against a wolf anyway? I must be crazy.*

She reached the room, her heart pounding wildly in her chest. Gripping the doorknob, Emily wondered why she heard no sounds in the house. No growling, no howling, no screaming in terror—nothing.

She took a deep breath, then another. She steadied herself, then she twisted the doorknob, thrust the door open, and burst into the room.

The door swung open faster than she thought it would. She lost her balance and tumbled to the floor, landing facedown. She rolled over, looked up, and found herself face-to-face with—Drew and Vicky.

The Strig kids both had puzzled looks on their faces as they glanced down at their friend completely sprawled out on the thick rec room rug.

Drew extended a hand and helped Emily up to her feet.

"Nice of you to come over," Vicky said. "I find that knocking on a door usually works better than somersaulting into a room. But that's just me."

Emily looked around the room in a panic. There was

no sign of the wolf and no evidence of a struggle or fight of any kind.

"Where did it go?" Emily asked, her heart still pounding.

"Where did what go?" Drew asked, looking at Emily as if she had three heads.

"The wolf!" Emily cried. "I saw it from my bedroom window. It came right through the front door!"

"You were spying on us from your bedroom window?" Vicky asked.

"No!" Emily protested, growing frustrated and more than a little confused. "I heard a howl coming from outside. When I looked out the window, I saw a big wolf. And it had blood on its fangs. It looked right at me and growled. Then it just walked into the house. I thought you guys were in trouble, so I ran over."

Drew and Vicky stared at Emily. Vicky raised her pencil-thin eyebrows and opened her eyes wide.

"Guys!" Emily moaned, hearing for the first time just how crazy her own words sounded.

Then she remembered Mr. and Mrs. Strig.

"Your parents!" she cried frantically. "They said hello when I came in, but then didn't answer when I warned them about the wolf. Maybe it went upstairs. Maybe it got them."

"Whoa, calm down," Drew said, extending his hands, palms out. "I'll go up and check to see if Mom and Dad have become wolf chow. Wait here."

Drew slipped out the door Emily had come through.

"So what were you doing when you heard this big bad wolf?" Vicky asked.

Great. She's making fun of me, Emily thought. "I was lying on my bed, listening to music. I got sleepy and decided to call it a night when I suddenly heard the wolf howl."

"You were lying on your bed and you got sleepy?" Vicky repeated.

"Yeah."

"And what did you tell me you had been doing earlier in the evening?" Vicky asked, as if she was a lawyer cross-examining a witness.

"Watching a scary movie," Emily replied, realizing where Vicky was going with this line of questioning. Emily started to blush.

"And is it possible that there was a wolf howling in said movie?" Vicky asked, crossing her arms in front of her, really getting into the whole lawyer-interrogating-a-witness thing.

"Yes," Emily admitted, sighing.

Vicky spun quickly and began speaking emphatically to an imaginary judge. "And so, Your Honor, I suggest that the witness did not see a wolf, but had, in fact, simply dozed off and had a dream about the wolf she had seen in that movie! No further questions. I rest my case."

"All right, all right," Emily conceded. "When you put it that way, I suppose I could have dreamed it all."

Drew rushed into the room, red faced and panting.

"It's terrible! It's horrible!" he cried.

"What happened?" Emily shrieked, rushing to his side.

"The wolf ate Mom, but—but—it didn't like the way Dad tasted, so it spit him out," Drew said, dropping his chin to his chest. "Dad feels so rejected."

Then he lifted his head and smiled at Emily.

"I get it, guys," Emily said, shaking her head. "I fell asleep. I had a dream. There was no wolf."

"Oh, Mom and Dad say hi, by the way," Drew added.

Emily nodded.

"Tell them I say hi back. And now that I've totally embarrassed myself, I'm gonna head home and see if I can get to work on a better dream."

"Don't worry about it," Vicky said sweetly, her usual edge softening a bit. "It happens to the best of us."

"Thanks," Emily said, thinking how great it was that Drew and Vicky accepted her even when she made a fool out of herself.

"Watch out for the wolf," Drew said as Emily headed for the door.

"Cute, real cute," Emily said.

She stepped from the house, closing the front door behind her. As she walked away she heard the muffled sounds of Mr. and Mrs. Strig talking to Drew and Vicky. A few seconds later, she was quietly opening the door to her own house, breathing a sigh of relief that her parents hadn't noticed her being gone.

Back in bed, Emily tossed and turned a bit before finally drifting off. Her dreams, while not scary, were fitful, filled with a sense of unease. She kept finding herself in unfamiliar rooms, trying to figure the way out, but running into one locked door after another. A feeling of dread pulsed through the dreams like a faint heartbeat. The last thing she remembered before the dreams finally stopped was the distant, lonely cry of an animal.

CHAPTER 3

BLEEP! BLEEP! BLEEP! BLEEP!

A terrible noise filled Emily's ears. Her eyes shot open wide and she bolted upright in bed. Then she glanced at the alarm clock on the night table next to her bed, saw that it was seven a.m., and realized that this was the source of the hideous noise. She slapped the snooze button so hard that the clock tumbled onto the floor. Dragging herself from the bed, the horrible reality of the situation dawned on her. It was Monday morning and she had to get up for school.

Emily had tried all different ways of getting herself to wake up for school. At first she set her iPod to wake her up with music. But when the wake-up music started blaring, she would just drift back to sleep, falling into a new dream based on the tune she had selected to awaken her. Then she had her mother call up to her room, but that just resulted in a grumble, a moan, and another plunge into slumber. So, in time, Emily realized that it had to be this loud, incredibly annoying clock that forced her up and out to start her day.

The weekend had flown by so fast. After she'd played beach volleyball with her dad all day Saturday and eaten way too much saltwater taffy yesterday, Friday night's wolf incident had pretty much faded from her mind. When it did circle back into her thoughts, she alternated between recalling just how real it had seemed and just how dumb she'd felt when she realized that it had only been a dream.

Emily got dressed, gulped down a bowl of cereal, and hurried off to catch the school bus. As the bus pulled into the school parking lot, she spotted Ethan Healy and Hannah Young, her two best friends. The three of them had been in school together since kindergarten. Here in middle school, they were not in all the same classes, but they always ate lunch together.

"Hannah! Ethan!" Emily called out as she bounded from the bus. "Wait up!"

"Hey, Em!" Hannah shouted back as the three friends fell into step together, heading for the school's main entrance. Hannah had short brown hair and a round face. When she smiled, her eyes twinkled mischievously, as if she was cooking up some kind of scheme. Hannah would do anything for Emily, and Emily felt the same way. Whoever came up with the abbreviation "BFFs" most definitely had Hannah and Emily in mind. "How was the beach?"

"Did your weird neighbors come with you?" Ethan jumped in, stepping in front of the two girls and walking backward.

Ethan was taller than Emily and Hannah. He had a mop of bright red hair that hung down into his face and shook when he walked. His hair was definitely the first thing anyone noticed about him, but it was his sense of humor that Emily and Hannah knew best.

"They didn't, but I did hang out with them on Friday night, Mr. Smarty Pants," Emily said. "They happen to be really awesome. But you wouldn't know that since you've never met them."

"Well, I met them, Em," Hannah piped up, "when I went with you to their house a couple of weekends ago. I usually like anyone you like, but they were kind of cold to me. And that house—I was really creeped out by that place."

"I know," Emily said. "But Hannah, you get spooked by butterflies, remember?"

"How could anyone forget?" Ethan chimed in. "You were the best part of our class trip to Butterfly World. From your reactions, you would have thought that you were being attacked by flying zombies or something, not little butterflies with pretty wings."

"All right, all right, are you guys done?" Hannah asked, shaking her head. "Am I ever going to live that down?"

"Nope," Ethan said matter-of-factly.

"Butterflies disturb me," Hannah continued. "All that fluttering around my face—ugh! Anyway, that doesn't have anything to do with what we were talking about."

"What *were* we talking about?" Ethan asked.

"Drew and Vicky," Emily reminded him.

"Right," Hannah said. "I was creeped out by their house. And I don't see what's so great about them anyway."

"They're nice and fun to hang out with, that's all," Emily explained. "You just have to give them a chance."

Before Hannah could reply, the bell rang, signaling the time when all students had to be inside.

"See you guys at lunch," Emily said, scooting into the building with her friends, who each went in a different direction.

Emily hurried down the hall. The last thing she needed was another tardy caused by standing outside the building, yakking away with Hannah and Ethan.

The rest of the morning dragged on, as Monday mornings always did. Emily made it through math, English, and gym. Lunchtime finally arrived.

As she headed to the cafeteria, she thought about what Hannah had said before school. So Hannah was a little creeped out by Drew and Vicky's house. So what? She shouldn't hold that against them. Emily wondered how she could get her friends to like one another. Invite everyone over all at once? Emily smiled to herself. A party wasn't a bad idea.

By the time she reached the cafeteria, the usual lunchtime pandemonium was well underway. She filled her tray, then deftly navigated her way between tables of screaming and laughing kids, ducking under a few flying trays and stepping around the odd container of spilled milk or splattered glob of Jell-O.

Spotting Hannah and Ethan at their usual table in the

corner near the window, Emily slid into a seat beside them.

"What'd you get?" Ethan asked, leaning forward, sticking his face right over her tray and scanning it, like a hungry hawk searching for prey on the ground below.

"Get your nose outta my food!" Emily said, gently shoving Ethan's forehead away. "I got the lasagna. It's the usual gloppy cheese, dried-out sauce, and some green things that perhaps were once vegetables."

"I got the meat loaf," Ethan said proudly. "I like not knowing what's in my lunch."

"You are so strange," Hannah chimed in, looking right at Ethan and picking up a forkful of salad.

"You've been saying that since we were six!" Ethan complained.

"Well, it doesn't make it any less true," Hannah shot back. Then she turned to Emily, as Ethan picked apart his meat loaf. "How was gym?"

"Rope again. Need I say more?"

"I know! If people were meant to climb ropes—"

"We'd have wings, right?" Ethan interrupted.

"What's that supposed to mean?" Hannah asked.

"Well, you know, so we could fly up the rope instead of having to climb it?" Ethan explained. The girls started giggling at the thought of Ethan with a pair of wings.

"Well, at least you won't have to climb the rope for too much longer," Hannah began. "The school year's over in just three more days, not counting today or our random day off on Thursday."

"What are we going to do to celebrate the end of the school year this weekend?" Ethan asked. "We could go to Ride World again. That was great—especially seeing your face on the roller coaster, Em!"

"As I recall, Ethan, I was not the one who lost his lunch when the Ferris wheel got stuck with us at the top," Emily replied.

"So I learned that I don't like heights," Ethan said defensively. "And that fried chicken sandwiches with peanut butter on top don't like me. That's a mistake I won't make again."

"I have a different idea for this year," Emily said, trying to steer the conversation back to reality and away from the strange planet known as Ethan's brain. "I was thinking we could have a big party. I'm sure I could talk my mom into letting us have it at my house."

"Ooh, fun!" Hannah squealed. "We haven't had a big

party in forever. Wait a minute. How about making it a sleepover?"

"An end-of-the-school-year sleepover party!" Emily cried. "I love it! Hannah, you are a genius!"

"I've been telling you that for years," Hannah said, hiding her face behind her hand, adding, "Please, no autographs."

"And that will be a perfect chance for you both to get to know Drew and Vicky better," Emily added. "You'll see that they're really cool."

"Wait," Hannah said, dropping her genius routine and staring at Emily. "You're going to invite them to our sleepover?"

"Yes," Emily replied quickly. "They *are* my friends."

"But they don't even go to our school," Ethan pointed out.

"They don't even go to *any* school," Hannah added.

"All the more reason to invite them, then, isn't it?" Emily asked. "This will be a chance for them to meet all my other friends, to help them feel like part of the gang. It's got to be hard when your parents homeschool you. It'll be a great time for everyone to get to know each other."

"Well, I don't—," Hannah started.

"Great, then it's settled," Emily continued, not allowing Hannah an opportunity to protest. "I'm glad we all agree."

"You're forgetting one thing," Ethan said, inhaling the last crumbs of his meat loaf. "I'm a boy."

"Really?" Emily replied in mock surprise. "I just thought you were a really weird-looking girl."

"Seriously, Em," said Ethan, rolling his eyes. "Hello! There's no way your mom will allow a coed sleepover!"

"Good point," Emily said, a bit surprised that she had completely overlooked this fact.

"How about the boys have to leave around ten or eleven?" Hannah suggested. "It can be a regular party, and then the boys can go home and the girls get to stay for the sleepover."

"That'll work!" Emily said, greatly relieved. "Hannah, you're—"

"—a genius, yes, we've already established that."

"Good idea, Hannah," Ethan said. "I'll bring the fried chicken with peanut butter sandwiches!"

BRIIING!

The bell rang ending lunch period, and the three friends got up, cleared their trays, and headed from the cafeteria with the stampede of the rest of the students.

"Call me tonight and we'll start planning the party!" Emily said to Hannah as the three friends headed off to three different classes. "See ya, guys."

Emily was bursting with excitement as she hurried off to history class. *Hannah and Ethan are going to love Drew and Vicky,* she thought. *The five of us are going to have the best summer together—and it all starts at this party. I can't wait!*

CHAPTER 4

"How was school today, honey?" Emily's mom asked as the family sat down for dinner that evening.

Emily glanced at the clock and saw that it was 7:55. *We're eating early tonight,* she thought as she dug into her dinner. *For us, anyway.*

"It was okay," she replied to her mom. "You know, the usual. Lunch with Hannah and Ethan, surrounded by a few classes."

"Funny," her dad said. "I guess I don't have to ask what your favorite subject is."

Since they were on the topic of lunch and Ethan and Hannah, Emily thought this might be a good time to mention the plan they had cooked up. She didn't think it would be a problem, but after all, there could be no party without her parents' permission.

"So, Hannah, Ethan and I were talking at lunch," Emily began. "You know, about what to do for the end of the school year?"

"How about finish your schoolwork and get good grades?" her dad suggested.

"I mean, *after* we do all that, Dad," she replied, smiling. There had been a time when her dad's dumb little jokes would have really bothered her. She took it as a sign of her ever-growing maturity that she could ignore them—like Mom always did.

"Another trip to Ride World?" her mom asked.

"Nah, we talked about that, but we wanted to do something different this year," Emily explained.

"How about a thrilling outing to Miniature Golf Palace?" her dad chimed in. "They have eight different courses, and you haven't lived till you've played them all twice."

Emily's mom gave her a look and smiled. "Here we go again."

"I aced the clown-face course," her dad continued. "Every hole is a different clown face. Put the ball in the last clown's mouth and his nose lights up!"

"Actually, we were thinking of having a party," Emily said, cutting right to the chase before the entire evening slipped away. "A sleepover party."

"Oh," said her mom, thinking this over. "Where? Here?"

"Of course," Emily said quickly. "You guys are the best. You know Hannah's parents are super uptight about everything, and Ethan's grandmother has an apartment in his basement so there's nowhere for us to hang out. Plus, everybody's so comfortable here."

"Everybody except Drew and Vicky, it seems," her mom said. "Will you be inviting them to the party?"

"Sure," Emily said. "I really want all my other friends to meet them."

"Well, that's fine, but I would really like to officially meet them and their parents, especially if they're going to be sleeping over in my house," her mom said.

"Well, Vicky will," Emily corrected her. "Drew and Ethan and any other boys who come will have to leave at some point, of course."

"Well, yes," her mom said.

"And you'll meet Drew and Vicky and their parents, I promise," Emily said, hoping she could keep her word. "Speaking of which, I told them I would go hang out tonight. See ya at nine thirty."

"Have fun, honey," her mom said as Emily got up from the table.

"I still think Miniature Golf Palace is a great idea!" her dad shouted as Emily slipped out the door.

A few minutes later Emily was in the Strigs' rec room, strumming on an electric guitar.

"Ready to rock out?" Drew asked, cranking up the volume on his amp.

"I'm just ready to try to keep up with you guys," Emily said, tuning the final string on her guitar.

"All right, enough talk," Vicky said. "Here we go. One-two-three-four!"

Counting off the tune, Vicky began bashing out power chords on her guitar. Emily, who was still a relative newcomer to the instrument, did her best to follow the chord changes as Vicky sped through the song.

Meanwhile, Drew played lead guitar, his fingers flashing up and down the fret board. He played a run of superfast notes, then bent some very high notes until it sounded as if the strings would pop right off.

As she struggled to keep up, Emily continued to be impressed by how well it seemed these two did everything. The first song ended, and Emily felt good that she had at least known how to play all the chords that Vicky was strumming.

"Wow! You guys are really good," Emily said, catching her breath. "I know it seems like I say that every time I come here, but it's true."

"We do get to practice a lot," Drew said.

"It comes with hanging out at home most of the time," Vicky added.

Emily took this as an opening. "So, about that. What would you say about coming to a sleepover party at my house this Saturday?" she asked.

"We'd have to check with our mom," Vicky replied. "She's a little weird about stuff like that."

"Stuff like what?" Emily asked.

"Sleeping over other people's houses," Vicky replied. "They like us being home."

"Well, here's the thing," Emily continued. "It's an end-of-the-school-year party and I really, really want you guys to come. My friends Hannah and Ethan will be there, and I'd love for you to get to know them so we can all hang out together this summer. Drew, all the boys have to go home around eleven, but Vicky, you can stay over."

Drew and Vicky looked at each other. They seemed to be genuinely surprised by Emily's announcement. They also looked slightly confused.

"It's nice of you to ask us," Drew finally said after an awkward few moments of silence.

"Of course," Emily said. "But the thing is, my mom wants to meet you and your parents first, you know, like now, before you come for the party, so the sooner you can convince your parents to say yes, the better it will be."

"I'll talk to them later," Vicky said. "They're busy now."

"How are they putting up with our loud guitar playing?" Emily asked, smiling.

"They love it," said Drew. "Seriously. And speaking of which, let's play another tune."

The trio broke into another song, and Emily was blown away by how Drew seemed to get better with each note he played. *He's better than half the musicians I hear on the radio,* she thought. *And he's only a kid. He has a chance to be a pro when he grows up.*

Again, Emily pushed herself. She could almost feel her playing improve as she concentrated intently. The song ended, and Drew gave her a high five.

"Nice!" he said. "You are getting so much better, Emily. We should go on the road!"

The road? Emily thought. *This guy isn't even allowed to leave his house!*

"Just kidding!" Drew said quickly. "Want to do another?"

"Sure, but first I need to use your bathroom," Emily announced. She pulled the guitar over her head and placed it on its stand. Then she headed for a door on the far side of the rec room.

Emily reached out to open the door.

"Don't open that!" Vicky cried out in panic.

Emily jumped in fright, pulling back her hand as if she had just received an electric jolt. "I'm sorry!" she said automatically, her heart still pounding in her chest, though she couldn't figure out what she had done wrong.

"No, *I'm* the one who should apologize, Emily," Vicky said, looking more pale than usual. "I didn't mean to have such an extreme reaction, and I didn't mean to scare you. It's just that that bathroom is broken and it has to be fixed. The last time someone went in there and used it, water went everywhere and the whole house was flooded for a week."

"You could go outside and pee in the woods behind our house," Drew suggested, flashing a big smile. "That's what I do."

Emily grimaced. "Gross! You sound like my friend Ethan. I'll just wait until I get home."

"So, Ping-Pong?" Vicky asked brightly. "I owe you a chance to get revenge for the foosball games on Friday night."

"Sure, why not?" Emily said.

The two picked up paddles from the Ping-Pong table set up in the corner of the room and began to volley back and forth. Drew continued to pluck out riffs on his guitar while the two girls smacked the ball over the net.

Emily held her own for a while. But then Vicky seemed to shift her game into a higher gear and put her away, winning easily.

"It's a good thing I really like you guys," Emily said, tossing her paddle onto the table. "Otherwise I would hate you for being so good at everything."

"You'll get there," Vicky said.

"Nice of you to say," Emily sighed. Glancing at her phone, she noticed that it was 9:20. "I think I'll head home a couple of minutes early and shock my mom when she sees me without having to text me to tell me what time it is. And I also gotta . . . well, you know." She gestured toward the door to the broken bathroom.

"Okay, so your homework, young lady, young man, is to work on your parents," Emily said, doing her best impression of a grown-up voice. "Then you all have to come over and meet mine. And then you can come for the sleepover and meet my friends. It'll be a great start to an awesome summer! See ya."

Emily headed over to her house. She hoped that maybe her little jokey encouragement would get Drew and Vicky to convince their parents to let them come over. Just before she reached her own front door, she heard a faint sound coming from across the street.

A-hooooo! Ow-ow-w!

She stopped short, the blood seeming to freeze in her veins.

"The wolf!" she whispered to herself. "That's the same howl I heard the other night. And now I know I'm awake."

A-hooooo! Ow-ow-w!

The sound came again, and this time Emily could pinpoint where it was coming from: the woods behind the Strigs' house.

"I've got to find out if I'm imagining things or figure out what in the world is going on here." She hurried back across the street, slipping past the Strigs' front porch, then circled around behind their house. Pausing for a moment at the edge of the thick grove of trees, she plunged into the dark woods.

"What am I doing here?" Emily wondered aloud as she picked her way past craggy branches, her feet crunching on fallen leaves and dried-out twigs.

Deeper she went, feeling the darkness close in all around her.

Something ran right past her. She actually heard the sound of something tearing through the woods a split second before she saw the streak.

"Yah!" she screamed, backing up and crashing into a tree.

Whatever it was flashed past her again, then disappeared, swallowed up by the darkness and silence.

Was it the wolf? Where did it go?

Deciding not to wait around to find out, Emily turned and ran. The woods were not very big, but panic made her doubt her usually reliable sense of direction. No. She was not about to get lost in the tiny woods she had been playing in since she was a little kid.

"Ah, there's the exit," she said to herself, breathing a sigh of relief. "And I can see streetlights between the leaves."

Just before she stepped out of the woods, Emily caught sight of something fluttering in the breeze up ahead.

"What is that?" she wondered aloud. When she got close enough to see, Emily gasped in horror. She was staring at a tuft of fur dangling from a tree branch—wolf fur—covered with blood.

CHAPTER 5

Emily put her head down and ran, her legs pumping, her arms shoving branches out of the way. She crashed through the last bit of woods that stood between that tuft of fur and safety, bursting out onto the sidewalk.

Glancing back over her shoulder toward the Strigs' house, she wondered if Drew and Vicky had heard the howling this time. Maybe they even had seen her running in fear from the woods she knew so well. Or maybe they saw whatever she had spotted running through the woods. But their house was dark. There was no sign of her two friends.

Emily dashed across the street to her front door and then paused.

Gotta catch my breath, she thought. *Can't let Mom*

and Dad see me all freaked out like this.

She wiped the sweat from her forehead with her sleeve and pushed her hair back into some sort of order. Then she took a deep breath and reached for the front door.

"Everything's fine. Everything's fine," she whispered, hoping this mantra would calm her down. "Everything's—YAH!"

She was startled by the text message alert coming from her cell phone—her mother's curfew reminder. She opened the door and stepped into her house.

"I almost beat your text tonight," she said, forcing a big smile—maybe a bit too big. "I was right outside the door when I got it."

"Everything okay, honey?" her mom asked. "You look . . . Did something happen tonight at Drew and Vicky's?"

"Nothing out of the ordinary," Emily replied, trying hard to pull herself together. "You know, we, uh, played guitar, then Vicky whipped me at Ping-Pong. The usual."

"Did they ask their parents about the party?"

"They're working on it, Mom," Emily said, heading for the stairs. "I'm pretty beat. I'm gonna head up to bed. G'night."

"Okay. Good night, honey. You sure everything's okay?"

"Peachy!"

Peachy? Emily thought as she bounded up the stairs to her bedroom. *I never say "peachy." Where'd that come from?*

Stretched out on her bed, she wondered if she was losing her mind or if there might actually be a deadly creature roaming around her neighborhood. And what exactly was it? A wolf? Not that it ever would have happened, but what if she had followed Drew's advice and went out to pee in the woods?

Then she remembered that the first time she'd heard and saw the wolf at the Strigs' door, porch lights all along the block came on as if others had heard it too. She could check with some neighbors. Maybe they remembered that night. But that was just a dream . . . or was it?

These questions kept her tossing and turning until she finally drifted off to sleep. Once again her dreams were filled with anxiety, though when she woke up Tuesday morning she could not remember any of them.

That morning in school Emily felt distracted. She

had not told Ethan or Hannah about the wolf incident from Friday night, figuring it was just a dream, despite how real it seemed. Now, after last night, she really wanted to tell them, but she also knew just how strange it was going to sound.

She debated with herself all morning, barely hearing what her teachers were saying and thankful that none of them called on her during any of her classes. As she walked to the cafeteria, Emily knew what she had to do. These three best friends had never kept secrets from one another—which was one of the reasons they had remained best friends for so many years—and now was not the time to start.

"I have some great ideas for the sleepover," Hannah said as Emily sat down at their usual lunch table.

"Me too!" Ethan added, flashing his partly jolly and partly demented grin.

"Seeing how far we can throw rolls of toilet paper from the upstairs windows hardly qualifies as a sleepover activity," Hannah pointed out.

"My brother's friends did it," Ethan grumbled, shrugging.

"That was for Halloween, Ethan," Hannah pointed

out. "And as I remember, more than a few angry neighbors stopped by the next day."

"No angry neighbors, please," Emily said, glad for the momentary distraction, but still bursting to tell her friends what had happened.

"So, here's what I came up with," Hannah continued.

"Hannah, before you tell me your ideas, I have something to tell you guys," Emily said.

"No! The party's canceled. Your mom said no, your dad—"

"No, no, no, the party's on. This has nothing to do with the party." Emily took a deep breath, then went on. "Last Friday I had this dream, or at least I think it was a dream. It's all so confusing now."

"Dreams usually happen when you're asleep," Ethan volunteered.

"Thanks for that valuable piece of information," Hannah said. "Now let Emily talk."

"So anyway," Emily continued, "I had been hanging out with Drew and Vicky. I went home and was on my bed when I heard howling. It sounded like it was coming from outside. I went to my window and saw . . . well, I saw a wolf!"

"A wolf?" Hannah asked in disbelief.

"Like a real wolf? Not like a big dog or something?" Ethan added.

"Yes, a real wolf," Emily said. "It was huge and horrible and had bloodstains on its mouth and teeth."

"They sell a special toothpaste for that now, you know," Ethan joked.

"Ethan!" Hannah shouted.

"I saw the wolf go into Drew and Vicky's house," Emily continued. "I panicked and ran across the street to save them."

"Wait, you went into the house?" Hannah asked, grabbing her head with her hands. "You thought you saw a bloodstained monster go in and you thought it was a good idea to just follow it and what? Fight it with your bare hands?"

"I know, I know. It's nuts," Emily said, sighing. "I don't know what I was thinking. But just let me finish, because it gets weirder."

Ethan leaned forward, placing his elbows on the table and resting his chin in his hands. "Weirder is good," he said. "Go on."

"Okay, so I followed the wolf into the house, but it

wasn't there. Drew and Vicky were there, just hanging out. They didn't hear or see any wolf. And I found no evidence that the wolf was ever there. When I told Vicky all about this, she convinced me that I had fallen asleep on my bed, dreamt all about the wolf, then woke up and ran over to her house. And that made sense."

"Sounds about right," Hannah said, shrugging. "So can I tell you about my party idea now?"

"Not yet," Emily replied, holding up her hands. "It did make sense, and I had pretty much forgotten about it, until last night."

Ethan leaned in even closer.

"I was playing some music with Drew and Vicky. When I left their house to go home, I heard the howling again. This time it was coming from the woods behind their house. So I went into the woods."

"Wait! Time out!" Ethan said. "You heard this wolf a second time and followed it again?"

"That's right."

"Okay, I have just one question, and it's a simple one. ARE YOU COMPLETELY INSANE?"

"Ethan, I had to find out. I had to know."

"And what did you find, Em?" Hannah asked, starting

to take this whole thing seriously for the first time.

"Well, I didn't exactly see the wolf. But I did see something moving very fast through the woods."

"Like a bunny?" Ethan asked.

"This was no bunny," Emily continued. "It was big, but it flashed past me so quickly, I couldn't see what it was. I was starting to run home when I saw a bloody tuft of fur hanging from a tree. It looked like wolf fur."

"Really?" Hannah asked skeptically. "Are you sure it had blood on it?"

"Pretty sure," Emily replied.

"I think maybe you're starting to get spooked from hanging around with Drew and Vicky all the time," Hannah said.

"I think Hannah's right," Ethan added. "Maybe hanging around with those two has got you seeing stuff. I mean, a fox, yeah, but there aren't any wolves for, like, a hundred miles."

"I guess you're right," Emily sighed. "But what's been making that howling sound?"

"It was probably just a neighbor's dog or something," suggested Hannah.

"And the bloody fur—that could have come from

anywhere," Ethan assured her. "Maybe two squirrels got in a fight."

Emily let out a deep breath. "Thanks, guys. I'm probably just making too big a deal out of nothing."

"Forget about it for now," Hannah said. "Let's talk about something fun, like my idea for the party—make-your-own ice cream sundaes!"

"I love it," Emily said.

"Excellent," Hannah said. "Now, for games I—"

The bell sounded, ending lunch period.

"Games will have to wait," Emily said. "Can't be late for history. We'll talk later."

"See ya," Hannah said, grabbing her tray and hustling from the table.

"Don't talk to any wolves on the way home, Em, okay?" Ethan added.

"Good-bye, Ethan," Emily replied.

As she walked to class, Emily found her thoughts turning back once again to the wolf. Despite her friends' reassurances, something didn't seem right to her. She just couldn't let it go. And even though Hannah didn't like them, she wasn't ready to give up her friendship with Drew and Vicky. She wanted them all to come to the sleepover. She was sure that once they all had some fun together, away from that creepy house, Drew, Vicky, Hannah, and Ethan would become friends.

But first she had to find out, once and for all, whether there really was a wolf or if she was simply losing her mind.

I'm going back into the woods tonight, Emily decided. *And this time I'm taking Drew and Vicky with me!*

CHAPTER 6

"So the sleepover party is definitely happening?" Vicky asked that evening when Emily went over to hang out. Vicky had just finished beating Emily in a game of Ping-Pong. They were each stretched out across a different tattered, overstuffed chair with their legs dangling over one of the chair's thick arms and their heads resting against the other. Drew looked on from the corner of the room, where he was restringing his guitar.

"Yep, everything's on," Emily replied. "My friends and I always do something special at the end of the school year. Last year we went to an amusement park. This year we thought a party would be fun and a sleepover party would be extra fun. What'd your parents say? You guys allowed to come?"

"I'm not sure," Drew said, never taking his eyes off the neck of his guitar. He tightened a string, then pulled another one from the package.

"What do you mean?" Emily said. "I thought you guys wanted to come. You know, since you don't go to school, this is a way you can be part of a group of friends."

Vicky looked at her brother, then at Emily. "We do want to come," she said. "It's just that we haven't been able to nail our parents down about going over to your house."

"Why not?" Emily asked. "You know my mom won't let me officially invite you to the sleepover until she's spent more than two minutes with you. And she'd really like to meet your parents, too. What's the problem?"

"You know, they're weird," Vicky replied, slightly defensively. "Lots of people have weird parents. I mean, are *your* parents totally normal?"

Emily shook her head. She couldn't figure out what the big deal could be with Mr. and Mrs. Strig, but it wasn't worth pushing too hard and risking her friendship with Drew and Vicky. "No, of course not," she said. "My parents are weird just like everyone else's. I mean, the other day my dad asked if he could come over with me and play foosball with you guys. And when I told him about the idea for the sleepover, he suggested we go play miniature golf instead. He is *such* a weirdo!"

Vicky and Drew both laughed.

"Anyway," Emily continued, "there's something else I wanted to talk to you both about."

Vicky sat up. Drew continued working on the guitar's sixth and final string.

Emily went on, "Last night, when I left your house, almost as soon as I stepped out, I heard—I heard—oh, boy, I just realized how weird this is going to sound. Well, I heard the wolf again."

Vicky's eyes opened wide. "The wolf from your dream?" she asked.

"It sure sounded like the same one," Emily explained. "But I didn't actually see it."

Drew put down his guitar and walked over to the girls. "Well, at least we know you weren't dreaming."

"Unless, of course, you were sleepwalking when you were over here."

"Vicky!" Emily cried.

"Just a joke. So what did you do when you heard the wolf?"

"Well, the sound was coming from the woods behind your house," Emily began.

"Really?" Drew interrupted.

"Without a doubt," Emily said.

"That's strange," Drew said. "I didn't hear a thing."

"Me neither," Vicky added. "So what did you do?"

"I went into the woods to see what was going on," Emily replied, as if it were the most natural thing in the world. "I know, you're going to say, 'Are you crazy, going into the woods by yourself to find a wolf—a huge, man-eating monster?'"

"No," Vicky said. "Actually, what I was going to say was that you're pretty brave for doing that and I wish I had been there with you. Sounds like a cool adventure."

"Oh," Emily said, pleasantly surprised.

"Did you see anything in the woods?" Drew asked.

"Nothing I could identify. I saw something big move very quickly past me. Then I heard the howling again. I got scared and ran from the woods. That's when I saw something hanging from a tree."

"What?" Vicky asked.

"Fur from an animal. A wolf maybe. And it was covered in blood."

"You're not making this up to get back at us for making fun of your dream, are you?" Drew asked.

"If it really was a dream," Emily said with renewed conviction that maybe she *had* seen a wolf that first night. "And no, I'm not making it up. In fact, I think we should go back out into those woods right now and find out once and for all if there is anything creepy and dangerous lurking in there."

Drew and Vicky looked at each other. They both shrugged.

"Let's do it," Drew said, setting his guitar onto a stand and heading for the back door.

Outside, the night was quiet. The three friends hurried across the unkempt lawn and paused at the edge of the woods. Emily nodded to the others, then continued ahead into the darkness.

Leading the way, with Drew and Vicky close behind, Emily moved quickly but carefully through the thicket of trees and bushes. She shoved aside branches and squeezed her way around thick tree trunks.

Emily stopped short in front of an old tree with sharp bare branches sticking out on all sides. "This is it," she said. "I'm sure of it. This is where the bloody tuft of fur was."

A bright light suddenly blazed to life, sending Emily stumbling backward, crashing into a tree.

"Who's there?" she cried.

"Um, sorry, it's just me," Vicky replied, waving a flashlight around. "I guess I should have warned you that I was turning on the flashlight, huh?"

"Yes! No surprises, please! We're in the woods, in the dark, hunting a monster, remember?" Emily screamed in an adrenaline-fueled shriek. She had been keeping her composure pretty well considering all this wolf-and-blood-and-creepy-woods craziness—until that moment.

She took a deep breath. "Okay, maybe I overreacted a bit. Anyway, now that you've got that thing on, shine it at the tree."

Vicky trained the flashlight's beam on the bare tree. She lit up the branches, moving her light up and down. Emily examined each branch. She saw no sign of the fur she had seen the night before.

Finding nothing on that particular tree, the trio moved deeper into the woods. The night was still. Even the usually fluttering leaves made no sound in the windless darkness.

"So what are we looking for now?" Drew asked, ducking under a branch.

"I don't know," Emily replied. "Something. Anything. Whatever it was I saw last—"

The sound of footsteps tearing through the woods stopped Emily short.

"Here it comes!" she whispered. "It sounds like what I heard last night. But I don't see anything."

The woods grew silent again for a moment, then the sound returned.

"Whatever it is, it's running through the dead leaves on the ground, kicking up a storm," Drew said, staring into the darkness, trying to find the movement that went along with the rustling and running sounds.

"There!" Vicky said a few seconds later, aiming the flashlight at the ground. The brilliant beam picked up a scurrying movement.

"That's it!" Emily cried, relieved to learn that she was not imagining things. There really was something out there.

The creature froze in the intense circle of light, then turned and flashed its dark eyes right at Vicky.

"Um, Emily, that's a raccoon," Drew said.

The small creature stared up at the friends, looking

at first puzzled, then annoyed. When it flashed a set of sharp-looking teeth, Vicky turned off the light, allowing the critter to go about its nocturnal business in private.

"*That's* what this was all about?" Vicky asked. "A raccoon in the woods at night?"

"No!" Emily snapped defensively. "I don't know. Maybe we should just—"

A-hooooo! Ow-ow-w!

Emily stopped talking and clutched Vicky's arm. "That's the sound—the exact sound, I swear," she said in horror. "It's the wolf! Shine your light! Shine your light!"

Vicky fumbled clumsily with the flashlight, trying to turn it on as quickly as she could.

Emily's frantic insistence didn't help. "Come on! Come on!" she cried.

A-hooooo! Ow-ow-w!

The howling came again, closer this time. Vicky dropped the flashlight onto the ground.

"It's getting closer!" Emily whispered.

Vicky dropped to her knees. She began to feel around desperately among the leaves and twigs. Emily knelt down beside her and helped with the search. If they were going to get torn apart by a wild beast, the least they could do was see the thing.

"Got it!" Vicky cried after a few more seconds of panicked searching.

A-HOOOOO! OW-OW-W!

The howling was right upon them now. Vicky lifted herself to one knee and flipped the switch. Her light blazed to life, and she aimed the beam right at the sound, which now seemed to be directly overhead, ready to pounce down onto them.

A-HOOOOO! OW-OW-W!

In the circle of light casting skyward, perched on a thick branch, stood an owl. The bird cocked its head as it peered down at the kids looking up at it.

"*A-HOOOOO! OW-OW-W!*" the owl screeched again. Then it spread its wings and took off into the night.

"Well?" Vicky said questioningly to Emily. "Seen enough? Do you need any more proof that there is no wolf, no monster, no bloodthirsty beast?"

Emily sighed. She still could not explain all this, but she also couldn't continue to search for something that most likely did not exist. "Yeah, let's go home. Sorry, Vicky. Sorry, Drew."

But Drew didn't respond. "Drew? DREW?! Vicky, where's Drew? He's gone."

"Drew!" Vicky called out.

"Drew!" Emily cried, their voices echoing through the trees.

"What are you two yelling about?" Drew said suddenly from behind them.

"Where were you?" Emily asked sternly, like a frightened mother reprimanding a child.

"I had to pee," Drew explained. "Did I miss anything?"

"You missed Emily being attacked by a killer owl. *A-hooooo! Ow-ow-w!*" Vicky did a pretty good impression of the owl.

"That's it, guys," Emily said, throwing her hands into the air. "I'm done with all this wolf stuff. I promise. I'm sorry I dragged you out here."

"It's no big deal," Vicky said. "It's a nice night for a walk."

Vicky had barely finished her sentence when the first drops of rain began to fall. The trio picked their way back through the woods. By the time they emerged into Drew and Vicky's backyard it was pouring.

"Sorry again, guys!" Emily said through the teeming

raindrops. "I'll see you soon." Then she ran across the street.

Pausing under the awning at her front door, she glanced back at the Strigs' house. She saw Vicky slip through the front door. Then she heard the all-too-familiar howling again. Leaning to one side to get a better angle on the woods, Emily saw something running—something larger than a raccoon or an owl.

She turned quickly away. "No," she muttered to herself just before stepping inside. "I am done with all this wolf stuff!"

CHAPTER 7

Emily tossed and turned, trying to force herself to fall asleep. She knew it was hopeless.

"I'm done with all this wolf stuff. I'm done with all this wolf stuff," she kept repeating over and over, hoping that she could convince herself it was true, or at the very least use it to help her fall asleep; kind of like counting sheep or listening to music.

No luck. The more she tried to push the weirdness out of her mind, the more it clawed at her. Sure, she could put on a brave face to Drew and Vicky and Ethan and Hannah, saying things like "I know it was only a dream," and "Yes, I love scary movies, and yes, I know I have an active imagination." But in her heart, she didn't buy it. Not for one second. There was something strange going on in her neighborhood, across the street, in the woods beyond the Strigs' house.

And at that moment Emily knew for certain that she had to find out what it was. She had to do this by herself, and she had never been surer about anything in her life. Jumping from her bed, she quickly got dressed. She glanced at the clock and saw that it was three forty-five a.m.—no time for anyone in their right mind to be getting dressed and going outside for any reason, much less to search for a monster.

Then again, Emily was far from sure that she was still in her right mind.

A-hooooo! Ow-ow-w!

The howling drifted through her window, as if somehow the creature knew that she was coming after it, and calling her to join it. Emily found it strange that this sound didn't scare her. In fact, it didn't even surprise her. She felt as though she had an appointment with the beast to settle their score. To end this.

Moving swiftly but as quietly as she could, Emily hurried down the stairs and slipped out the front door. She had never been outside this late before. There was that time when she was nine, her family had to make a trip to visit a sick aunt, and her dad decided it would be better to drive all night than to fly out the next day. But other than that and a few restless nights before big tests, Emily had never really seen what three forty-five a.m. looked like. But now she was out in it.

Her safe, comfortable neighborhood felt odd. The quiet was startling. No cars, no music or TV sets, no one mowing the lawn. Only her footsteps tapping against the blacktop as she crossed the street.

Without pausing, she walked right onto the Strigs' front yard, went around to the back of the house, and reached the edge of the woods.

A-hooooo! Ow-ow-w!

"I'm coming," Emily said boldly. "And I'm not afraid of you."

Emily had been in these woods so many times that she felt she could almost find her way around blindfolded. And she might as well have been, given how dark it was. Fearlessly she pushed through the thick branches, annoyed at their latest attempts to scratch her. She couldn't see or hear the wolf, but she felt she knew exactly where to go to find it.

Deeper and deeper she plunged until she came to a

slight clearing that she somehow knew was right in the center of the woods. Emily looked in every direction, peering into the dense growth just beyond the small opening in which she stood.

"Where are you?" she muttered. "Show yourself. Show me that you are real!"

Snap.

A small twig snapped behind Emily. She spun around and spotted a thick, hairy paw emerging from the undergrowth. The paw was followed by a leg, then the wolf's large head and long jaws slid out from the thicket.

The creature turned its head sideways and narrowed its eyes, as if it were sizing Emily up. She stood her ground. She had not come this far to turn away now. Emily had never felt so brave. She met the wolf's gaze with a penetrating stare.

The wolf drew back the skin around its mouth, revealing the same bloodstained teeth Emily remembered from the first time she had seen the animal—in that so-called dream that clearly was no dream.

Crouching low, the wolf let out a deep, low-pitched growl. Brave as she was trying to be, Emily began to feel afraid . . . very afraid. The creature seemed to sense this change of emotion, from her rock-steady conviction to the overwhelming fear that now threatened to hold her paralyzed where she stood.

That's when the wolf sprang forward, charging at Emily, its eyes wild with rage, its jaws wide open, trailing long strings of blood-flecked saliva.

Emily turned and ran, crashing back through the dense woods. She gave no thought now to being brave, or to proving to everyone else that the wolf was real. Her only thought was to survive.

Branches tore at her face and arms as she ran. No matter how fast she pushed herself, she could hear the wolf close behind. Its powerful legs pounded into the ground, propelling the beast forward, growling and snarling as it ran.

Emily's ankle caught a low branch. A jolt of pain shot through her leg as she tripped and tumbled to the ground, twisting and landing on her back. The wolf increased its speed, seeing that its prey was vulnerable now. It leaped into the air, ready to come down right on top of her.

In the split second that the wolf was airborne, Emily

rolled over, the pain in her back and shoulders matching the ache in her ankle. The wolf slammed to the ground beside her, landing just inches away from her face. It slid along the fallen leaves and twigs and crashed into the base of a tree.

Emily pushed herself up from her stomach and stumbled forward, shoving the pain aside. Behind her, she heard the wolf scramble back to its feet and continue its close pursuit.

Jumping over low branches and ducking under higher ones, Emily maneuvered through the woods like some combination gymnast and high-hurdles track star. Ahead she spotted a thin ribbon of light through the trees. She allowed herself to feel hopeful.

The streetlights! she thought. *I'm almost there, almost home.*

Emily emerged from the woods into the Strigs' backyard. She glanced toward the door, hoping that maybe the noise from the chase would have awakened someone.

The Strigs' house was dark and still.

She glanced back over her shoulder. The wolf was still just a few feet away.

Dashing across the street, Emily made for her front

door, like a runner sprinting for the finish line. Her legs felt like lead, her ankle throbbed, and she began to tremble as she ran.

The wolf drew closer and closer.

Emily hit the front steps and took them two at a time. She grabbed the front door, threw it open, and ran inside. But the beast was right there, leaving her no time to close the door and keep it out.

She bounded up the stairs, but the wolf was right behind her, nipping at her heels. If she could only make it to her room. But what about her mom and dad? Even if she could make it to safety, the wolf would surely get them.

Trying to force herself to move faster, Emily stumbled on the top step and hit the landing, sprawled out on her back. The wolf was next to her in a flash, its paw on her shoulder, pinning her down.

The wolf lowered its jaws toward her face and began to change shape. While becoming no less menacing, it morphed into a human shape.

As the creature came closer, Emily got a good look at its face—its human face.

She was stunned.

The face was shockingly familiar. She knew this face. But who? Whose face was it?

The human monster still had long fangs, which it now lowered toward Emily's neck.

CHAPTER 8

"Yaaaiiii!" Emily screamed, bolting upright in bed, covered in sweat. She flung the covers off and rolled to the floor to get away from the monster attacking her. Then she realized that there was no monster. She was alone. It was not three o'clock in the morning, but rather seven a.m. The shine was shining. Sitting on the floor, panting, out of breath, Emily slowly realized that she had just had the worst dream of her life.

"The whole thing, the howling, the woods, the chase, the changing from a wolf into a person—it was all a dream, a long, terrible dream," Emily muttered to herself. She looked down and saw that she was sitting on the floor beside her bed, completely tangled up in her blankets. "Okay, Emily, first . . . get up off the floor."

She rolled to one side, then pushed herself up, tossing the blankets back onto the bed in a heap. Sitting on the edge of her bed, she tried to make sense of the crazy nightmare. She felt as if someone had been shaking her and shaking her, refusing to stop. The actual events of the previous evening slowly came to her, as if a fog in her head was lifting. She could once again begin to distinguish between reality and the dreamworld in which she had been spending far too much time lately.

Emily remembered searching the woods for real—she believed—with Drew and Vicky, and finding nothing. Nothing except for a few small animals that belonged there. She recalled deciding that she had had enough of all this wolf business and vowing to put it out of her mind. But apparently her mind had other plans.

It's one thing to believe you saw a wolf strolling through the neighborhood, Emily thought as she tried to remember what day it was. *At least that is possible, even though it's not very likely. But a wolf shape-shifting into a person?*

She had read enough science-fiction books and seen enough scary movies to think that the idea was pretty cool. But the "fiction" part of "science fiction" meant that it wasn't real! And whose face was that in her dream anyway? She couldn't recall any details other than the overwhelming feeling that this person-monster-thing was someone she knew.

"Emily! Are you up? Breakfast is ready!" her mother called from downstairs.

"Be right down, Mom!" she yelled back. Emily knew she had better get moving before she missed the school bus.

Hurrying through her shower, Emily tried to wash away the sickly feeling that still lingered from the dream. After dressing quickly, she bounded down the stairs, looking forward, more than usual, to the normal, boring breakfast chitchat that she sleepwalked through most mornings. She, of course, had decided to tell no one about her dream.

Slipping into her chair at the breakfast table, Emily began shoveling spoonfuls of cereal into her mouth.

"So how's the sleepover planning going, honey?" her mom asked.

"Okay," Emily replied, guzzling down a glass of orange juice. "Hannah and Ethan have come up with some pretty good ideas for the party. Well, Hannah has, anyway."

"Well, you just be sure to let me know if there's anything I can do to help. I used to love sleepovers when I was your age."

"Thanks, Mom."

"What about Drew and Vicky?" Emily's mom asked.

Emily felt herself tense up. Her mind shot back to their expedition in the woods and then to her horrible dream.

"What's the matter, honey?" her mom asked.

Emily quickly realized that her expression must have changed.

"Did you and Vicky have a fight or something?" her dad asked, looking up from his phone.

"Have you invited Drew and Vicky to your party yet? Are they planning on coming?" her mom added.

"No, no, we didn't have a fight," Emily answered her father. "Sorry, my mind wandered for a second. I did invite them, and I really hope they come. But they haven't had a chance to talk to their parents. Mr. and Mrs. Strig are kind of funny about Drew and Vicky going anywhere. I guess that's why they're homeschooled."

At that moment, Emily felt as if a lightbulb had switched on in her brain. "Homeschooled!" she repeated. "Of course. That's it."

"That's what?" her mom asked.

"I've been going about this all wrong," Emily said. "I've been overlooking the obvious. I'm the one who has to talk to Mr. and Mrs. Strig about Vicky and Drew coming over. They work a lot of nights and weekends, but they have to be home during the day because Drew and Vicky are homeschooled."

"O-kay," her mom said slowly, raising her hands and shaking her head.

"Don't you see?" Emily asked, smiling as her dream begin to fade from her mind. "We have no school tomorrow. Some end-of-the-year teacher conference thing, but for Drew and Vicky it'll just be another regular day of homeschooling—with their parents! I'm going to go over there tomorrow and ask them if it's okay for Drew and Vicky to come to the party. And I'll invite the whole family over to meet you and Dad tomorrow night. It's perfect!"

Emily jumped up from the table and grabbed her books. "Bye, Mom. Bye, Dad," she said, kissing each of them. "Thanks!" Then she hurried toward the door.

"You're welcome?" her mom replied questioningly, wondering exactly what Emily was thanking her for.

That day at school was a bear for Emily. Not only

did she have two finals scheduled, but her math teacher sprang one last pop quiz on the class as well. By the time she got to lunch, she was completely stressed.

"Em!" Hannah called out from their usual table. "We've got some serious party planning to do."

"Can't," Emily said, pausing at the table but not sitting down at her usual seat. "Gotta cram for the history final. It's on the Civil War."

"The North won," Ethan volunteered, being his usual helpful self.

"Seriously, guys, I gotta study, but no worries. We're off tomorrow, remember? So let's hang out, okay?"

"I have my first soccer practice for the summer team in the afternoon," Ethan said.

"And I've got to watch my little brother when he comes home from morning preschool," Hannah added.

"So let's hang out in the morning," Emily suggested. She knew that she had to go talk with Mr. and Mrs. Strig tomorrow. But there would be plenty of time to do that in the afternoon. After all, her parents didn't get home from work until late anyway.

"Okay with me," Ethan said. "You wanna meet at the lake?"

"Sure," Hannah said. "Ten?"

"Great. See you guys then."

Emily slid into a seat at an empty table and pulled out her history book. She hardly ate any of her lunch, cramming Gettysburg and Appomattox into her brain rather than mac and cheese into her belly.

When her excruciating day finally came to an end, Emily was exhausted. She had planned to maybe go play guitar with Drew and Vicky that evening, but she felt herself dozing off at the dinner table. She watched about ten minutes of *Attack of the Zombies*, a "true classic" as she described it to her parents, then headed up to her room.

Emily checked her e-mail to see how many of her friends had RSVP'd to her party invitation. Two additional people said they would be coming, bringing the total so far to twelve. This was going to be a great party, but at the moment, all Emily could think about was going to bed. She slept like a rock and had no dreams, scary or otherwise, that she could remember.

The following morning she had the great pleasure of sleeping until she woke up on her own. She had remembered to turn off that annoying pest known as her alarm clock. Her parents were long out of the house by the time she stirred. She fixed herself a bowl of cereal, which she ate while watching the rest of *Attack of the Zombies*. Then she took a shower, threw on some clothes, and hopped on her bike.

During the twenty-minute bike ride from her house to the lake, Emily's mind focused on the sleepover. She had been so consumed with studying for her tests, not to mention all this wolf nonsense, that she had hardly had any time to really think about the party, which was now just two days away. She was really looking forward to kicking around some ideas with Ethan and Hannah. Then later in the day she would finally officially meet Mr. and Mrs. Strig and work it out so that Drew and Vicky could come to the party. It was all good.

Coasting down the final hill approaching the lake, Emily saw that Hannah was already there. She slowed to a stop beside the dock, then lowered her bike to the ground.

"Hey, Em," Hannah said, tossing a small rock into the water and watching the ripples spread out. "How was the history final?"

"I think I did okay," Emily replied. "The North won, right?"

"Cute!"

"Who's cute?" asked a voice from behind them. Ethan crouched down at the edge of the dock and dangled his feet just above the water. He lived the closest to the lake of all three friends and could easily walk there.

"You are, Ethan," Hannah said, blowing silly exaggerated kisses at him. "Don't you think so, Em? Ethan is *sooo* cute."

"Guys!" Emily cried, holding up her hands. "Please, no flirting. I just ate."

"Okay, down to business," Hannah said. "Here's what I have in mind for the sleepover. We all agreed on make-your-own ice cream sundaes."

"Check," Emily said.

"For a theme—"

"A *theme*?" Ethan interrupted. "We need a theme for the party? How about summer's here and everybody hangs out and has fun? Is that a good theme?"

"It's so sad, Ethan, really," Hannah said, the fake sympathy practically dripping from her voice. "You obviously know nothing at all about throwing a successful party."

"Oh yeah?" Ethan said defensively. "Well, one time Roger, Chuck, Sid, and I ate so much kettle corn and drank so many milk shakes that Roger ended up puking all over Chuck's bathroom. And Sid had to go the hospital to get his stomach pumped. Now *that* was a fun party."

"Delightful," Hannah said. "Sorry I missed that."

"Yeah, me too," Emily added. "Be sure to send me an invite the next time you guys decide to test the limits of the human stomach."

"Okay, back to my theme," Hannah said. "You ready? Camping out, indoors! We set up tents in your home theater. We eat dinner sitting around that DVD your parents have of a fireplace burning."

"Ugh, that thing," Emily said, scrunching up her face. "My dad insists on putting it on every Christmas."

"But you guys have a real fireplace," Ethan pointed out.

"Please. Don't I know it," Emily said. "But you know my dad. He thinks the fire looks so real in HD that he insists on playing it every year. It's so silly."

"But for us, it can fill in as our campfire," Hannah jumped in. "Sleeping in tents, eating around the fire."

"Making s'mores in the microwave!" Emily chimed in, starting to get excited about the idea. "And—oh, this is great!—we can tell scary stories! Just like a real campout. Hannah, I'm loving this!"

"Have you been getting replies to your invite?" Hannah asked.

"Yup, we're up to twelve, including you guys," Emily reported. "My mom said she'd like to limit it to about fifteen."

"Oh, I know what I wanted to tell you, Em," Ethan said, picking up a stick and poking it into the water near a school of small fish. The tiny minnows scattered, moving as a group. "My cousin Declan will be visiting me the weekend of the party. Okay if I bring him along? He's pretty cool, like me."

"I don't know if we could handle two kids who are as cool as you, Ethan," Hannah joked, playfully poking Ethan in the ribs.

"Sure, you can bring Declan, no problem," Emily replied. "So that brings us to thirteen."

"Does that include Drew and Vicky?" Hannah asked.

"No, not yet. I'm hoping that they'll fill in the last two spots."

"What's taking them so long to get back to you?" Ethan asked.

"They haven't been able to get their parents to give them permission to come," Emily explained. "But all that is going to change." She told her friends about her plan to talk to Vicky and Drew's parents later that day. "I'm telling you, after today, everything with Drew and Vicky will be different. You'll see. You'll like them."

CHAPTER 9

Satisfied with their party planning, Emily, Hannah, and Ethan left the lake, heading their separate ways. Hannah hurried home to watch her little brother, and Ethan ran off to the school for soccer practice.

As Emily rode her bike home she began to get excited, but also nervous, about her plan to barge in and introduce herself to Drew and Vicky's parents. In the months she'd been hanging out at Drew and Vicky's, she'd called up to them a bunch of times, but she'd never actually met them face-to-face. What was she going to say to them?

"Hi, Mr. and Mrs. Strig. I'm Emily Hunter," she rehearsed aloud as she pedaled toward home. "I'm your neighbor, you know, from across the street. The house with the green shutters and white—"

Emily smiled to herself. *They don't need a detailed description of your house. They'll know who you are. You've been hanging out there, like, every day for the past few months.*

She tried again. "Hi, Mr. and Mrs. Strig. I'm Emily Hunter, you know, Drew and Vicky's friend? You've probably heard me playing guitar with them? I hang out at your house sometimes?" *Jeez, Em, just get to the point!*

"Mr. and Mrs. Strig, I would like to invite you and Drew and Vicky to my house so you can meet my parents. And I would also like Vicky and Drew to come to my sleepover party on Saturday. Well, Vicky will actually be the one sleeping over. All the boys will be leaving at eleven and —"

Emily sighed. *Forget it. You'll figure out what to say when you get there.*

A few minutes later she turned into her driveway and slowed to a stop. Leaning her bike against the garage door, she took a deep breath and walked quickly across the street.

Emily climbed the lopsided steps leading onto the Strigs' porch and walked across the creaky floorboards to the front door. Then she knocked on the door.

No reply.

Again she knocked. Again, no sound from within.

"Maybe they're in the back of the house. Of course, if they had a doorbell . . ."

Emily thought about turning around and going home, but she knew she would regret it. She'd gotten herself psyched to do this and she would not get another chance before the sleepover.

She grabbed the ancient doorknob and turned it. The door squeaked open with a pitiful groan.

"Drew, Vicky? Is that you?" a woman's voice said.

"We're upstairs," added a man's voice.

Why aren't Drew and Vicky home being homeschooled? Emily thought.

"Mr. Strig! Mrs. Strig! It's Emily Hunter from across the street. Drew and Vicky's friend. May I come in and talk with you?"

The Strigs remained silent.

What is with these people?

Emily backed up onto the porch and closed the front door. *Should I just go home?* she wondered. *But I can't chicken out now. I just need to go upstairs and talk to these people. After all, they're just people, right? What can they do, bite my head off?*

Emily opened the door again.

"Drew, Vicky? Is that you?"

"We're upstairs."

Now Emily was really confused. Wasn't that the same thing they'd called out when she came in the first time? And why hadn't they answered her when she called up to them? And that's when it hit her. She'd heard Mr. and Mrs. Strig say the same thing each time Drew or Vicky opened the front door. She closed the door, then opened it again.

"Drew, Vicky? Is that you?"

"We're upstairs."

"Okay," Emily muttered. "What's going on here?"

She opened the door fully and stepped inside.

Instead of walking straight down the hallway, as she always did to go to Drew and Vicky's rec room, Emily turned left. She followed the narrow hallway around a curve and came to a large wooden staircase. It had obviously once been a grand stairway fit for a mansion. She could picture a bride walking down its long sweeping stairs, trailing the train of her wedding gown behind her.

But, like everything in this house, the staircase had fallen into terrible disrepair. Emily carefully adjusted her weight as she took every step, making sure that each stair would support her before she committed fully to moving up onto the next one. Every stair moaned as if it resented being used after so many years.

Reaching the landing, Emily found another hallway, similar to the one on the first floor. This hallway also looked as if it had been thrown together quickly using some unpainted Sheetrock that someone had just found sitting around. At the end of the hallway, a single door stood closed.

"Mrs. Strig?" Emily called out in the direction of the closed door. "Mr. Strig?"

No answer.

Reaching the door, she knocked, her raps echoing into the room beyond.

Emily psyched herself up. "Just do it, Em. Open the door."

She nodded to herself, then opened the door and stepped into the room.

Somehow the fact that the room was practically empty did not surprise Emily. The walls had long ago crumbled. Pieces of plaster lay scattered on the floor, exposing the beams that held what was left of the house together. A single piece of furniture, a small table, sat in the corner. But what was that on the table?

Crossing the room carefully to avoid falling into one of the many holes in the floor, Emily reached the table. Inspecting the small, square device on it, she realized that it was an old-fashioned telephone answering machine, the kind people used before voice mail.

A cassette tape sat inside the answering machine. Emily had seen these types of answering machines in movies from the 1980s. She pressed a button labeled OUTGOING MESSAGE. The cassette tape rolled, and two voices came out of the machine's tiny speaker.

"Drew, Vicky? Is that you?"

"We're upstairs."

When the message finished, Emily saw the tape rewind so it was ready to play again when the next phone call came in—or in this case, the next time someone opened the front door.

Emily walked completely around the table and discovered a wire coming out of the back of the answering machine. She followed the wire down to where the wall met the floor. From there it ran toward the door.

Tracing the wire, she followed it out of the room, along the hall, and down the stairs. At the bottom of the staircase, the wire crossed the floor and ran up to the door hinge, where it disappeared into a small plastic box. Emily pulled the cover off the box and found two batteries inside. The answering machine's wire was wrapped around a metal post. A second wire led from the box to a small speaker mounted on the wall at the top of the stairs. This was obviously where the message came out when the door was opened.

Emily sat down on the bottom step, trying to make sense of what she had just seen. For some reason, Mr. and Mrs. Strig had set up a phone answering machine to play their voices whenever anyone opened the door. But why? And where were they? They were supposed to be here, homeschooling Drew and Vicky.

Drew and Vicky. Where were *they*?

Emily got up and walked down the hall. Reaching the rec room door, she paused, then knocked.

"Drew? Vicky? It's Emily. I'm off from school today."

Silence.

She opened the door and stepped into the rec room. She saw the usual array of guitars and amplifiers, the foosball and Ping-Pong tables, but no Drew or Vicky. Again she called out. "Drew? Vicky?"

Again, no reply.

Emily had always known that there was something different about the Strigs. She knew that Drew and Vicky were not like her other friends. She wondered why Mr. and Mrs. Strig were being so weird about a simple thing like letting their kids hang out at a neighbor's house.

But this—this was more than she could make sense of. What about the whole homeschooling thing? If Drew and Vicky were not here getting lessons, then where were they? And what was the deal with the answering machine? Why were Mr. and Mrs. Strig trying to fool people into thinking they were home when they weren't?

WHERE WAS EVERYBODY?

Emily's mind raced in frustration. Then she spied the bathroom on the far side of the rec room—the door that Vicky had thrown a fit about when Emily had tried to open it. Her confusion and concern quickly gave way to a rush of curiosity. She crossed the room, grabbed the doorknob, and opened the door.

What Emily saw when she stepped through the doorway was almost more than her brain could comprehend. This was no bathroom. It wasn't even a room. It was an open expanse with a dirt floor, raw beams, and crumbling walls. The rest of the house, beyond the rec room, barely existed as anything more than a shell. Giant cobwebs filled every corner. Mice scurried along the dirt floor, pausing and sniffing, then resuming their search for food. A mass of insects crawled slowly, making the floor appear to be alive and moving.

Before Emily's mind could wrap itself around this sight, and just when she thought this whole thing couldn't get any weirder, it did. Sitting on the dirt floor were three long wooden boxes. As she moved closer, Emily's eyes widened in fright.

"C-coffins!" she stammered. "Three coffins!"

CHAPTER 10

Emily backed away from the coffins and stumbled, landing hard on the dirt floor, her face just inches away from a line of crawling bugs.

"Ah!" she screamed, scrambling to her feet. She ran back into the rec room, through the hallway, and out the front door. As she hurried across the street, she wondered for a second if she had remembered to close the front door and the door leading from the rec room to the room with the coffins.

The room with the coffins.

Nothing unusual about that, Emily thought. Just a typical suburban room with a dirt floor, cobwebs as big as SUVs, and the usual three coffins. It's all the rage this year. "What! You only have two coffins in your dirt room? Please. Everyone is going for the three-coffin look this season. I saw it on the cover of Better Homes and Coffins *magazine.*"

"Calm down, Emily," she said aloud. "If you are going to completely lose your mind, the least you can do is have the courtesy to wait until you are in your own home."

Emily threw open her front door and ran inside.

Good thing her parents were not home. Emily knew that there was no way she could hold it together and keep what had just happened from them. She slammed the front door shut, locked it, scooped up the cat for comfort, and then ran up to her room. She sat on her bed, then immediately got up and started pacing. Franklin watched her as she moved back and forth.

"How could I have been such a fool? Was I just impressed by how good those two were at everything? I thought Drew and Vicky were a little weird, but not *that* weird. There's a big difference between being a little weird and living in a house that's not really a house, having a coffin or three in a secret room that they were freaked out about me possibly discovering, with parents who only exist on a recording, and—"

Emily stopped pacing, lost in her thoughts. *Could it be that there is no Mr. and Mrs. Strig? That they died, and for* some reason Drew and Vicky don't want anyone to know, so they set up this complicated hoax? Do the coffins belong to Mr. and Mrs. Strig?

Emily started to turn green—this wasn't just creepy, it was downright gross. *Why? Why? Why? Why would you hide the fact that your parents are dead? And why three coffins?*

She sat back down on her bed and forced herself to take a deep breath. She really didn't know what was going on. She felt duped, taken, lied to. Whatever the deal was with Drew and Vicky, they were not who they appeared to be. Hannah had seen that there was something creepy about Drew and Vicky, but until now Emily couldn't see it. Or maybe she just hadn't wanted to.

Well, that was about to change. She was through with them. She didn't ever want to go back into that freak show of a house, and she certainly didn't want them in her house. It went without saying that Drew and Vicky would most definitely *not* be coming to her sleepover.

Emily snatched up her cell phone and started tapping out a text message to Hannah. She had no intention of telling anyone about what she had just seen, but she did want her other friends to know that Drew and Vicky would not be coming to the party.

HEY, HANNAH. THINGS DID NOT GO SO GOOD AT DREW AND VICKY'S. THEIR PARENTS REFUSED TO ALLOW THEM TO COME TO THE PARTY. THEY DON'T EVEN WANT ME TO HANG OUT WITH THEM ANYMORE.

Emily sent the message. A few seconds later she got a reply:

SORRY, EM. I KNOW YOU LIKED THEM (EVEN IF I DIDN'T!).

Emily wrote back:

THANKS. THE REALLY WEIRD PART IS THAT DREW AND VICKY DIDN'T EVEN SEEM TO MIND. GUESS I'VE SEEN THE LAST OF THEM. CU LATER. . . . E

Emily felt better that she had at least told Hannah something. She felt bad about lying to her, but she didn't know what to make of all this herself. She was not about to try to explain what she had seen to Hannah or Ethan or especially to her parents. She was too embarrassed about everything. She could say that she had gotten into a fight with Drew and Vicky. She could say that Mr. and Mrs. Strig didn't want their kids hanging out with her anymore. That would get her mom's back up. She would have a hard time believing that anyone wouldn't want their kids hanging out with her daughter.

Emily smiled at the thought of how loyal her mom was.

She began to feel a little better. The burden of trying to get Drew and Vicky to fit in with all her other friends, plus the pressure of getting the Strigs to meet the Hunters before the party, had obviously been weighing on her more than she realized. Having all that lifted off her shoulders felt like a real relief. Emily began to relax. She slid down, stretched out on her bed, and dozed off.

Bing-bong! Bing-bong!

Emily awakened to the sound of the doorbell ringing. She glanced at her clock and saw that it was eight fifteen. The sun had already set. She had slept the afternoon away.

Emily tiptoed down the stairs, dreading the two people she knew would be on the other side of the door. Franklin stood at the top of the stairs, hissing, his back arched.

"Emily, it's Vicky!" Vicky shouted as she began banging on the door.

"And Drew!"

"We finally talked to our parents, and it's okay. They want to meet your parents, and they're going to let us come to the sleepover party. Just open up and let us in."

Emily ignored them.

They pounded on the door. "Emily! Emily!" they called urgently from the other side. "Let us in! Please let us in!"

Emily felt a small pang of guilt. After all this time, Drew and Vicky finally wanted to come over. They wanted to come to the sleepover, and now she was the one resisting.

Then the image of the coffins popped into her mind, and a cold chill ran down her spine.

No. The friendship was over. Whatever was going on in that house, she had no intention of being part of it any longer.

Finally, after a few minutes, the knocking stopped. Emily peeked through the curtains and watched as Drew and Vicky headed back across the street and into their house.

Emily walked back up to her room and grabbed a funny book from her shelf. She just wasn't in the mood to watch a scary movie as she waited for her parents to get home.

When dinner was finally ready at nine o'clock, Emily slunk down the stairs and into her seat. She didn't even complain that dinner was especially late tonight. Her mother and father hadn't gotten home until just a few minutes before.

"You okay, honey?" her mom asked as Emily pushed some take-out pasta around her plate.

"I'm fine, Mom. I just don't think I'll be hanging out with Drew and Vicky anymore."

"Did something happen today?" her father asked.

Emily took a moment to gather her thoughts. She knew she had to tell her parents something, but she wanted to make sure that it was the same story she had told Hannah.

The last thing she wanted was to get caught lying to the people she cared about the most.

"Their parents said that they didn't want them to come to the sleepover," Emily said. "And the thing that upset me the most was that Drew and Vicky didn't seem to mind."

"I'm sorry, honey. That's no fun," her mom said. "But maybe someday Drew and Vicky will come around and you can all be friends again."

"I doubt it," was all Emily said in reply.

After dinner, in her room, Emily was listening to music, trying to put the unreal events of the day behind her. Her cell phone sounded with a text message alert.

The message was from Vicky:

HEY, EM, WHAT'S GOING ON? HOW COME YOU DIDN'T ANSWER YOUR DOOR? . . . V

A few seconds later a message came in from Drew:

EM, MOM AND DAD SAID OKAY. WE CAN COME TO THE PARTY! . . . D

Emily sat with her thumbs poised above her phone's keys. A hundred things she wanted to say flashed through her mind. Finally she tapped out:

WHAT'S UP WITH THE COFFINS?

She stared at the message and decided not to send it. She really didn't want to have anything to do with Drew and Vicky, starting right now.

But another message came in just a few seconds later:

ARE U MAD AT US? . . . D

"How do I answer that?" Emily wondered aloud. "I'm not mad at them, that's not it. I just don't really want to be friends with people living in half a house filled with coffins and parents who exist only on tape."

Emily knew that she had to send them some kind of

explanation. She typed out a new message:

I SAW THE COFFINS. PLEASE DON'T BOTHER COMING TO MY PARTY. YOU'RE NOT INVITED ANYMORE. LEAVE ME ALONE.

She sent the message.

A minute passed, then five, then ten. Emily dozed off an hour later, having received no reply from either Drew or Vicky. It was over. She'd let them know that she had seen the weirdness that was their life and wanted no part of it.

The following morning, Friday morning, the last day of school, Emily checked her phone. No messages. She could turn her full attention to the party, which was now only a day away.

CHAPTER 11

On Saturday morning Emily woke up and looked at her alarm clock.

"Six thirty!" she groaned. "That can't be right." She was wide awake, her brain buzzing.

On school mornings she could hardly drag herself out of bed at seven, and that was with her alarm set super loud. On weekends she barely budged before ten. But now here she was at six thirty on the first day of summer vacation, awake, alert, and positive that there was no way she was going to fall back asleep.

She threw off her covers and slipped out of bed. "Six thirty," she muttered. "Even the birds don't set their alarm clocks for this early."

Over breakfast, Emily ran through the checklist of

stuff she had to do that day. "Let's see—decorate the home theater, set up trays and bowls for munchies, go with Mom to pick up the pizza and ice cream."

Emily's mom drove her to several stores. By the time they got back, Hannah and Ethan had shown up to help with the preparations.

"I am so excited that this is really happening!" Hannah cried, hugging Emily.

"So we have to turn this house into a jungle?" Ethan asked as he stepped inside and looked around.

"Not a jungle, Ethan," Emily said, giving him a hug. He returned a halfhearted pat on Emily's back. "A forest. And not the whole house, just the home theater downstairs."

"Hello, Hannah, Ethan!" Emily's mom said, stepping into the entryway. "Thank you so much for coming over to help Emily."

"No problem, Mrs. Hunter," Hannah said. "The three of us cooked up this idea together, and we're going to see it through as a team."

"I came up with an idea for eating really gross food," Ethan said proudly. Then his expression soured. "But the girls voted it down."

"That's a shame, Ethan," Emily's dad said, joining the group. "I know that's always my favorite part of camping out."

"When did you ever camp out, Dad?" Emily asked skeptically.

"One time in college, when I locked my keys in my car and had to spend the night in a parking lot," Mr. Hunter said defensively.

"That's what I figured," Emily said, heading for the door leading down to the basement. "We've got work to do! See ya later, Dad."

"Have fun making your jungle," Mr. Hunter said.

"Dad! It's a forest!"

Hannah and Ethan followed Emily downstairs and they got right to work. In keeping with the theme of camping out, they took branches from trees that had recently been trimmed and hung them from the ceiling with clear fishing wire. They placed a few large potted plants around the room to act as the bushes. Emily then placed her collection of stuffed animals in and around the potted plants. The indoor wildlife included assorted bunnies, cats, and a polar bear.

"So, give me the details of what happened with Drew

and Vicky," Hannah said as she carefully placed a stuffed cougar into a tall plant to make it look as if the cougar was hiding as it stalked its prey.

"You know, Hannah, I don't really know," Emily said, feeling bad about continuing her fib. Maybe one day she would tell her friends the whole story. Or maybe not. What she did know was that if she told the whole story to them now, it would be all they could think about, and that would ruin the party for them. "I think it has a lot to do with their parents. Mr. and Mrs. Strig refused to allow Drew and Vicky to come to the party. They had no interest in meeting my mom and dad. But the thing that made me realize that Drew and Vicky were just not worth all the trouble was the fact that they couldn't have cared less that they wouldn't be coming to the party. In fact, it seemed to me that they didn't care about whether or not we were even friends."

"And who needs friends like that?" Ethan added as he placed the stuffed polar bear on the couch. "Especially when you have great friends like us who come over and help you set up a forest—er, complete with a polar bear."

Emily giggled. "Thanks, Ethan," she said. "You guys

are real friends. You'd never do anything to make me feel bad."

A short while later the decorating was all finished.

"This looks amazing!" Emily said, glancing around her former home theater and current private campground. "Thank you, guys, so much for helping."

"And now, I've got to scoot home and change for the party," Hannah said as the trio headed up the stairs.

"Change?" Ethan asked, sounding truly baffled. "I have to change?"

Hannah and Emily both turned around and stared at Ethan. He was dressed in a shirt that might have once had sleeves and a collar, but now looked like it stayed on Ethan's body only because it was too tired and tattered to care enough to fall to the ground. He wore gym shorts—last year's gym shorts, which were so faded the school logo was illegible. On his feet he wore sneakers with no socks. His big toe peeked out of the side of the left sneaker.

"No," Hannah said dryly. "You look fine." Then she and Ethan headed for the front door. "See ya tonight, Em!"

When Hannah and Ethan had gone, Emily went

back downstairs. The room really did look like a small forest. She headed back upstairs to help her parents prepare the food. Soon everything was ready. Now came the hard part—sitting around waiting for the guests.

CHAPTER 12

Six o'clock finally rolled around. The doorbell rang. Emily ran for the door, followed by her parents. It was Hannah, of course. Emily knew she would be the first guest to arrive.

"Welcome to the campout!" Emily cried, opening the door and giving Hannah a big hug, as if she hadn't seen her in months.

"Can you believe it's finally here?" Hannah squealed joyously. "This is going to be so great!"

"Nice to see you again, Hannah. Long time, no see," Emily's mom joked.

"Come on in," her dad added.

"Hi, Mr. and Mrs. Hunter," Hannah replied.

She gave each of them a quick hug. "Thanks again

for letting us use your house for the party."

"You know that Emily's friends are always welcome here," Mrs. Hunter said. "And you kids did a fabulous job decorating the downstairs."

"Yeah, it really looks like a forest," Mr. Hunter added. "I had to take my GPS with me when I went down there so I didn't get lost!"

Emily was in such a good mood that even her dad's corny jokes seemed funny today.

A few minutes later, the doorbell rang again. Emily opened the door and saw Ethan standing there with another boy. This boy was not as tall as Ethan, but his hair was also bright red, though he kept it shorter and neater than Ethan did.

"Em, this is my cousin, Declan," Ethan said. "Declan, Emily."

"Hey, Declan, come on in," Emily said. "Ethan, on the other hand, you can wait outside."

"You're very funny, as always," Ethan said. Then he followed Declan into the house.

"Thank you for inviting me, Emily," Declan said. "I know how much Ethan likes you."

"All right, all right!" Ethan said, pushing Declan

through the door. "That's enough of that Ethan-likes-you stuff."

Emily laughed. "Well, I really can't stand him," she said.

"Hi, Mrs. Hunter," Ethan said, handing a grocery bag to Emily's mom. "Here are the toppings for the ice cream sundaes."

"Thanks for bringing those, Ethan," Mrs. Hunter replied.

Over the next hour the remainder of the guests arrived. By seven fifteen everyone was down in the home theater and the party was in full swing.

As everyone munched on pizza, the talk turned to teachers the kids had this year and who they might have next year. Some kids talked about their plans for the summer.

"I'm off to Camp Cheapskate again in a couple of weeks," Roger Higgins announced.

"Is that really the name of the place?" Emily asked.

"Nah, it's really Camp Chesapeake, but everyone calls it Camp Cheapskate because the guy who runs it is so cheap," Roger explained. "His idea of a camp T-shirt is a white undershirt with 'Camp Chesapeake' written on it in Magic Marker."

"Sounds like my kind of place!" said Ethan.

"Ice cream time!" Emily's mom called out from the top of the stairs. "Make-your-own sundaes."

The kids all charged up the stairs, as if they hadn't eaten in a week. On the kitchen counter, Emily's mom had set up three flavors of ice cream, plus cherries, M&Ms, sprinkles, chocolate syrup, and a spray can of whipped cream.

One by one, the kids scooped ice cream into bowls, then tried to defy the laws of physics by cramming twenty ounces of toppings into a ten-ounce bowl that was already filled with ice cream.

Ethan picked up the can of whipped cream, shook it vigorously, then sprayed a stream right at Declan. Reacting as if he knew the whipped cream attack was coming, Declan ducked. The stream of white foam shot over his head and struck Roger in the face.

Rather than get mad, Roger picked up his spoon, scraped the whipped cream off his cheek, as if he were shaving, and shoved the spoon into his mouth.

One of the girls, Sarah Cooke, winced. "Em, what time did you say the boys were leaving?"

When everyone had finished their ice cream, the

kids all tromped back downstairs.

Emily pulled out a bunch of tents. "Time to go camping!" she announced. The girls each grabbed a tent and began to set them up, with the boys lending a hand occasionally.

The girls set their tents up in a circle near the TV, under the dangling branches. Then Emily popped in her dad's fireplace DVD, complete with a crackling fire in realistic surround sound.

"This is so dorky!" Ethan exclaimed.

"So it's perfect for you," Emily shot back.

Declan laughed. "I think it's cool."

"Thank you, Declan," Emily said. "You are welcome here anytime. Now who's got a scary story?"

"What kind of scary story?" Sarah asked.

"Any kind," Emily said, shrugging.

"How about monsters chasing people through the woods?" Ethan suggested.

"Or maybe a wolf chasing someone through the woods," Hannah chimed in, making a scary face and curving her fingers into the shape of claws. "Or how about a scary story about creepy neighbors?"

Emily shot a look of mild annoyance in Hannah's

direction. The last thing she wanted was to be reminded of her wolf hallucinations, or the Strigs.

"She's talking about Drew and Vicky, right?" Ethan asked.

"Right," Emily replied.

"Who?" Declan asked.

"Did you notice that creepy old house across the street when my mom dropped us off?" Ethan asked.

"Yeah."

"Well, the kids who live there are really weird," Ethan explained. "Or so I've heard. I've never actually met them."

"What's so weird about them?" Declan asked Emily.

"Oh, nothing," Hannah jumped in. "Just the way they're always together and the fact that they never seem to leave that house. The one time I met them, they never made eye contact with me. Not for one second. It was like they were somewhere else, even though we were in the same room."

"And their house is filled with all sorts of old, dusty things," Emily added.

That was all she would say. Just as she had promised herself earlier, she was not about to reveal the truth about just how weird Drew and Vicky really were.

"But enough about them," Emily continued. "Who has a scary story?"

"I do," Declan said. "It's a tale all about vampires."

"Cool, I love vampire stories!" Emily exclaimed.

"Me too," Declan said.

"Did you ever see *Vampire Babysitter?*" Emily asked. "That's one of my favorite movies."

"Only a dozen times," Declan replied. "It's a true classic."

"Agreed. So, what's your vampire story?"

Declan cleared his throat and began. "Five hundred years ago in a remote mountaintop village—"

"In Transylvania, right?" Ethan interrupted his cousin.

"In the Swiss Alps, actually," Declan explained.

"Ethan, no interrupting!" Emily scolded him. "Go ahead, Declan."

"This particular *Swiss* village," Declan continued, looking right at Ethan, "had been plagued by a series of brutal murders. Victims were found dragged from their homes, lying dead in the snow. All of the victims were bitten in the neck. But the odd thing was that some appeared to have been bitten by a person and some by an animal."

"So the murderer had a vicious dog that helped him," Ethan jumped in. Emily said nothing this time. Asking Ethan to stop interrupting was like asking him to stop breathing.

"Not necessarily," Declan went on. "Because as it turned out, these were no ordinary murders. They were the work of a vampire. The villagers knew this because one by one the bodies of the victims started disappearing from the cemetery. People started reporting seeing their dead relatives walking through the village at night."

"But what about the human and animal thing?" Ethan asked.

"Well, that was just further proof that the killer was a vampire. What most people forget is that vampires can shape-shift. They can change their form to look like other people, but they can also change themselves to look like animals. Some vampires actually prefer to hunt and feed in their animal forms."

"Like as a mean, vicious dog?" Ethan asked.

"A dog, maybe, but also a wolf or a jackal, or, of course, the classic bat."

"A hamster?" Ethan asked.

Hannah giggled.

"Not usually, no," replied Declan seriously, totally ignoring Ethan's joke. "Anyway, one day, during a particularly bad snowstorm, a local villager huddled in front of a blazing fire in his hearth. Shortly after the sun set, a sharp knocking came at his door, cutting through the constant howl of the wind outside. Peering out his window, the man spotted a stranger standing in the raging storm. He wore only a thin coat and no hat or gloves. He shivered and shook as snow piled up on his shoulders and head.

"'Please let me in,' the stranger cried. 'It's cold and I've traveled such a long way.'

"Now, the villager knew of the recent attacks, so he hesitated. Again the man outside pleaded with him.

"'Please let me in!'

"The villager had a good heart, and the man outside looked so cold and tired. He looked as if he couldn't hurt anyone. And so the villager opened the door. 'Come in and get warm, my friend, before you freeze to death.'

"As soon as the stranger was inside, he began to change shape. He grew taller and stronger-looking. Well, the villager was never seen again. When his friends came to see what had happened to him, they found one set of footprints leading up to the door, and two sets leading away."

"If the vampire was so strong, why didn't he just bust into the guy's house and bite him?" Ethan asked.

Declan shook his head. "He couldn't. If a vampire catches you wandering around outside, he can do as he pleases. But the only way a vampire can enter a person's home is if that person invites the vampire in. Otherwise the vampire cannot enter."

"That wasn't so scary," Ethan said.

"I liked it," Hannah said. "How about you, Em? You're the big scary movie fan." Hannah looked over at Emily. Her eyes were opened wide, and her face had turned pale.

"What's the matter, Em? I never figured you for one to get so scared by a story."

Emily's mind raced. She felt as if her brain was going to leap right out of her head. The story was set so long ago, but so much of it seemed . . . familiar. It all made sense now. Everything. The coffins, the wolf, never seeing Drew and Vicky during the day, the homeschooling, the fake parents, the way they pleaded to be let in once they decided they wanted—what? What did they want?

Oh no, I know what they wanted, Emily thought. They wanted someone to fill that third coffin. They wanted me. It's all so clear to me now. Mr. and Mrs. Strig weren't lying in those coffins. They don't even exist. Those coffins belong to Drew and Vicky, because Drew and Vicky are vampires!

CHAPTER 13

"I'm fine," Emily said, waving Hannah away. She struggled to regain her composure. She was not going to let this ruin her party. Besides, she had never let Drew and Vicky in. She was safe. She pushed all this craziness aside and invited someone else to share a scary story.

A couple of other kids told stories. One was about an alien abduction. Another, about the ghost of a sailor doomed to sail the seas forever.

The storytelling was interrupted by Emily's mom calling down from the top of the cellar stairs. "Okay, guys, it's eleven o'clock. Time for the boys to go home and for the girls to go to sleep. Ethan, your mom is here to pick up you and Declan."

"Okay, Mom," Emily called back up.

The boys said their good nights and thanked Emily.

"Another successful end-of-the-year event," Ethan said as he headed for the basement stairs. "Although not quite as memorable as puking at the top of the Ferris wheel."

"Thank you so much for inviting me, Emily," Declan said as he followed his cousin up the stairs. "I had a great time."

"You're welcome," Emily replied. "Thank you for the vampire story. That was great. I hope I get to see you again soon."

When the boys had all gone, the girls gathered in a tight circle and chatted about summer plans, what they might do at the end of the next year, and about how charming Declan was.

"Okay, girls, lights-out time," Emily's mom called down.

Emily turned off the TV, putting out their campfire, and one by one, the girls slipped into their tents. Just before she went into her tent, Emily glanced toward the basement window. There appeared to be a face peering in at her. She knew the face. It was Vicky!

She blinked and rubbed her eyes. When she opened them again, Vicky was gone. There was no one at the window. *It's been a long day*, Emily thought. *Just go to sleep.*

She crawled into her tent and slipped into her sleeping bag. She was exhausted from the day's events but was still wired from the excitement and the evening's startling revelation.

Vampires living across the street from her. Now that she thought about it, it sounded ridiculous. There had to be some logical explanation, right? There were no such things as vampires. But she must have believed it to some degree, since she felt so relieved that she had never officially invited Drew or Vicky in. And in the last text she sent them, she'd specifically told them they weren't invited to her party. Still, Emily thought about that third coffin and shuddered. She hugged the sleeping bag around herself tighter. Eventually she drifted off to sleep.

Emily's jumbled dreams were shattered by the sudden, jarring ring of her cell phone. She groped around the dark tent until she found her phone. "Who is calling at one eighteen in the morning?" she muttered to herself. Then she saw the caller ID.

She answered the call. "Ethan, are you out of your mind?" Emily whispered.

"Just listen, Em! Listen!"

Emily could clearly hear the panic in Ethan's voice. She had never, ever heard him sound like this. She knew that this was no joke.

"What happened, Ethan? What's wrong?"

"It's Declan," Ethan cried, his voice choking. "We found him."

"Found him?" Emily repeated, moving deeper into her tent, turning away from the flap and trying to keep her voice down so she didn't wake up anyone else. "What do you mean, found him? He left here with you and your mom."

"No, he didn't. He was never at the party. He was not at your house tonight."

"What? What are you talking about?"

"A little while after we got home, Declan said he had to go to the bathroom. He stayed in there forever, so I knocked on the door but got no answer. When I went in, I saw that he was gone and the bathroom window was wide open. I searched around outside, but he wasn't there. When my mom finally opened the hallway closet, she found him. He was unconscious and all tied up. He's okay, but he was really shaken up."

"Did he tell you what happened?"

"He said that shortly before we left for the party, while my mom and I were out at the store picking up ice cream toppings, someone grabbed him. Someone very strong. The next thing he knew, he was waking up in the closet when we found him."

"So then, who was at the party with you tonight?"

"I was," said a voice from behind Emily, startling her, causing her to drop the phone.

She had not heard anyone enter her tent. She spun around and there he was, looking down at her . . . Declan!

CHAPTER 14

"Who are you?" Emily gasped, her hand reaching instinctively to her neck. "Who are you?"

She watched in horror as Declan slowly changed shape. His features blurred, rippling like wax on a melting candle. Then the process unfolded in reverse. The wavy unclear face re-formed, and Emily found herself staring up at Drew.

"Drew!" she exclaimed.

Every instinct told Emily to run, to push past Drew and get out of that tent. Then her eyes met Drew's dark, penetrating stare. His eyes burned deeply into hers. Emily tried to scream, but her voice choked in her throat, as if invisible hands were clutching her neck. She tried to get up, but found she couldn't move. Some unseen force held her in place as panic rose up through her, filling her very being.

"Hello, my dear, dear Emily," Drew said, in a calm, soothing voice. "Thank you for inviting me into your house earlier this evening. Oh, I know you thought I was that boy Declan, but that doesn't matter. You invited me in, and as I explained to you earlier, vampires cannot come into a home unless they are invited in by the person who lives there."

Vicky suddenly appeared next to her brother in the tent. "Or if they are invited in by another vampire," she said, smiling down at Emily, adding her intense supernatural stare to Drew's.

Emily suddenly felt her panic ease. The edges of her vision blurred. Only the deep black circles of Drew's eyes remained in sharp focus. Everything else faded. An odd calm washed over her as she looked up and listened to the two oddly comforting voices.

"I know what you're thinking, Emily," Drew continued. "Why did we wait so long to come into your house? Why didn't we just make you a part of our family during one of the many evenings you were in our house?"

"We had to be sure," Vicky explained. "We had to spend time with you, to see if you were the one—the right one to spend the rest of eternity with us. You see, Emily, we like you very much. You are special, so special that when we met you, we considered expanding our little family for the first time."

All of this made perfect sense to Emily in her state of unnatural calmness. Strangely, she felt honored, even anxious, to join them. Some tiny part of her brain realized that the vampires' power included mind control as well as control over her muscles. But she didn't care.

"By now you have figured out that Vicky and I are not really brother and sister," Drew went on. "I wandered alone for centuries until I found one worthy of joining me."

"And now we have found another," Vicky said. "But it took a long time. That's why we were reluctant to come over to your house. We knew that once we were invited in we would take that opportunity to have you join us. You see, we don't like to leave the comfort of our house and our coffins, and when we do, it has to be for something very important. We didn't want to waste the chance before we were sure."

"Unfortunately, just at the time that we decided you were the one, you chose not to see us any longer," Drew explained. "And we are sorry you had to see your coffin before you were ready to enjoy it. Once you refused to come to our house anymore, we had to get you to invite one of us in."

"You feel at peace now, don't you, Emily?" Vicky asked. "You are ready. The time has come. And speaking of time, now you'll have all the time in the world to learn to beat me at foosball and Ping-Pong and learn to play every riff ever played on the guitar . . . and those that haven't even been created yet."

Vicky opened her mouth, revealing long, sharp fangs. She moved closer.

Emily was suddenly distracted by the sight of Drew slowly morphing again. This time he lost his human shape and changed into the form of a wolf—the very wolf she had seen again and again, complete with blood-specked fangs and a snarling growl. Then slowly the wolf transformed back into Drew, just as he had in Emily's dream.

It was Drew all along, she realized. He was the wolf. He left his house in this form to feed at night. Emily was so distracted by the astonishing transformation that she hardly noticed the sensation of Vicky's fangs sinking into her neck.

She felt a rush of warmth flood her body. The last bits of fear and apprehension washed away in a gentle wave. Then everything went dark.

EPILOGUE

The last rays of sunlight disappeared in smears of red and orange behind the distant mountain. As darkness blanketed the world once again, Drew and Vicky stepped from their house into the cool evening.

Years had passed since the night of the sleepover, and much had changed. Drew and Vicky no longer lived in the same town. As the two had done many times before, they moved to an abandoned house in a new town where no one knew them. Where they would be safe. And where they could make new friends.

"I'm certain about Billy," Vicky said as they kept to the shadows of their dark street.

"It's been a few months and he's come over almost every night," Drew remarked.

"And I agree with you," Vicky continued. "It's her turn. And he seems particularly drawn to her."

"Yes," Drew replied.

They walked up to a house just down the street from where they now lived. Vicky rang the doorbell.

A boy who appeared to be about Vicky and Drew's age opened the door.

"Hey, Drew, Vicky," said the boy. "What's up?"

"We realized that we've been friends all this time and we've never even seen your house," Vicky explained.

Billy looked around, gazing past Drew and Vicky. "Hey, where's your sister?"

"Right here!" called out a voice from behind Drew. "Have my brother and sister been giving you a hard time?"

"Hey, Emily!" the boy said, his face lighting up.

"Hi, Billy," Emily said. She flashed a big smile at him. "Can we come in?"

DO NOT FEAR—
WE HAVE ANOTHER CREEPY TALE FOR YOU!

TURN THE PAGE FOR A SNEAK PEEK AT

You're invited to a

CREEPOVER®

Ready for a Scare?

"They're not coming back," Ryan Garcia announced.

"What?" Kelly demanded. Gray slush from her boots fell in clumps onto the woven mat by the front door, leaving behind small pools of water. The warmth of the house felt good. The bus was like a freezer on wheels, and she was starving. Friday was Taco Day. So totally beyond disgusting, and of course, her mom hadn't packed her any lunch. For the last hour, she'd been thinking of nothing but the package of chocolate cookies waiting in the pantry.

"Mom and Dad," Ryan added.

Kelly kicked off her boots, and Ryan followed her across the front hall and into the kitchen. Her fuzzy blue socks slipped on the worn wooden floor. She dumped her backpack and hunter-green parka on one of the mismatched chairs, then turned to stare at her little brother. "What are you talking about?"

At ten years old, Ryan delighted in taunting her with secrets. His days were spent scheming to possess more information. As if it made him smarter or more grown-up. He still hadn't clued in: She didn't really care. Usually.

Ryan watched her open the pantry and grab the foil package. She slid out four cookies. They were the over-size, hockey-puck kind. Four seems like the right number to make up for lunch, Kelly reasoned. She ate the first one and let him wait. She knew he wanted her to ask again. To beg for more information. Ryan fidgeted, trying so hard not to tell her anything until she asked.

She ate the second cookie, chewing slowly. "So?" she finally said.

"So . . . we're all alone," Ryan reported. He looked unsure.

"Meaning?"

"Meaning Mom and Dad aren't coming back. Just like I told you."

Kelly studied her brother's face. He wasn't smiling or smirking. Had something bad really happened?

Her mind raced through the possibilities. Car accident. Plane crash. She grabbed his arm. "Ryan, come on. Tell me what's going on."

"Snowstorm," Ryan said, swatting her hand off his sweatshirt. "They're in Philly."

Kelly took a deep breath, annoyed that her brother had almost scared her. It was only for a second, but still. *That's my job*, she thought. *Everyone knows that I'm the best at scaring people.*

"When did they call?" Kelly asked, biting into another cookie.

"About ten minutes ago." Ryan grabbed a cookie from the package too. The elementary school bus got home before her middle school bus. Mom and Dad must have called just as Ryan let himself into the house. "There's a blizzard or something. They're going to call back."

And just at that moment, the phone rang.

"Guess that's them." Kelly hurried to the phone on her mother's desk in the far corner of the kitchen. Her mom referred to her desk as "Command Central." In the middle sat a huge calendar with all their activities, and scattered about were school directories, recipes printed from the Internet, magazines she hadn't yet read, and a whole mess of other papers. Kelly never understood what gave her mother the right to be on her case about cleaning her room when her desk was such a disaster.

"Hi," Kelly said, sitting on the wooden desk chair.

"Kelly, honey, I'm so glad you're home," her mother panted. She sounded strangely out of breath.

"Of course I'm home. Got to get ready for my party. Lots to do," Kelly reminded her.

"Oh, Kels." Her mother sighed. "Listen, about that. Daddy and I are stuck in Philadelphia."

"Ryan told me." She glanced above the desk at the enormous bulletin board covered with articles and downloads. Her mom, among a million other things, wrote a column for their weekly town paper called It Happened Here. It was about all the unimportant things masquerading as history that had happened in their little Vermont town since the French trappers first arrived. Kelly kept telling her mom no one cared. But the editors kept asking for columns. She guessed it gave the newspaper a reason to exist, because there was certainly no real news going on in her town. The bulletin board was like a mini history lesson, if anyone cared to read the columns, which she didn't. Kelly usually just read the photo captions while she was on the phone.

"It's snowing like crazy here. They canceled all flights out of the airport." Her mom sounded tired. She'd been up since dawn.

"What are you going to do?"

"We thought of renting a car, but the weather report says the storm is heading up the East Coast. A big nor'easter. Should be in Vermont by nightfall. The roads will be a mess." Kelly could hear her dad in the background, trying to tell her mom something. "The only sensible thing for us to do is to spend the night in a hotel here."

"Oh. Okay." Kelly had never stayed alone in the house overnight. She felt fine with it, though. She had babysat for little kids down the street, and that was no big deal. She could totally handle Ryan. Between the TV and his videos games, he'd stay out of her way. Besides, Paige and June were sleeping over tonight. An early birthday celebration. She'd have company.

"Daddy and I will leave first thing in the morning to get back home," her mom promised. Kelly could hear the worry in her voice. "What, Dave? How can they not have rooms? Look, the meeting wasn't my brilliant idea. It's fine . . . whatever . . . anywhere . . ." Her mom argued with her dad in the background. They had a company together, Authentic Vermont Blankets. Supposedly there was something about the sheep in their state that made superior wool for blankets—or at least, that was what her parents advertised. They had flown to Philadelphia this morning to try to convince some big store to sell their wool blankets instead of Amish quilts.

Kelly peered at a photocopy of a news clipping on the bulletin board about a woman named Mary Owens. She had never noticed this one before. The picture showed a young woman wearing a mod 1960s minidress and tall white patent-leather boots. A one-of-a-kind homemade necklace was draped about her neck. She sat serenely on a sofa, a playful smile on her thin lips. A Christmas tree decorated with candy canes filled the space behind her.

Her mom sighed. "Your dad could only find us a room in some ramshackle motel." Kelly could hear other voices and the muffled reverberations of loudspeaker announcements. She guessed they were still at the airport. "Kel, listen. I need you and Ryan to stay put. No going outside. And lock the doors."

"Sure." She studied the perfect swoosh of Mary's chestnut hair across her forehead. She wondered if her shoulder-length dark-brown hair could do that too. Doubtful.

"Chrissie is coming over at six," her mom continued. "She's bringing a pizza for dinner."

Kelly tore her gaze away from pretty Mary Owens. "Chrissie Cox? Why is she bringing us dinner?" Chrissie was her best friend Paige's older sister.

"Chrissie will be staying with you and Ryan tonight."

"A babysitter?" Kelly cried. "You got us a babysitter? I'm way too old for a babysitter! I'm in middle school."

"I know how old you are," her mother said. "But I'm not leaving you and your brother overnight alone. It's not safe. Plus, a big storm is coming."

"But Mom, we won't be alone," Kelly reminded her. "Paige and June are coming for the sleepover."

"Kelly, that can't happen tonight. Not without me or your dad there."

"That's not fair! It's not my fault there's a storm. It's my birthday!" Kelly cried.

"No, it's not," Ryan piped in behind her.

She shot him an evil glare. He crossed his eyes at her. "Real mature," Kelly muttered.

"We'll move your birthday celebration to next weekend," her mother said. "Besides, your birthday is really on Tuesday," she rationalized, as if Kelly didn't know when it was. "So next Friday will work just as well."

Kelly groaned. Typical of her mother. She always moved holidays to suit her own schedule. They often had Thanksgiving on a Sunday so her mother's whole family could drive in, and Easter on a Saturday so they didn't have to fight the weekend traffic home from Boston.

"But—" She had planned so many great things for tonight.

"No buts, Kelly. I'm counting on you. I'll call back when Chrissie gets there," her mom said. "Dad and I need to find this motel before the roads become impassable."

"Okay." She sighed. She wasn't happy, but she didn't have a choice. She knew that. No sleepover. She passed the phone to Ryan. As he babbled about some science project in school with pennies and sugar water, Kelly took a closer look at Mary Owens. The caption under the picture said the photo had been snapped at a Christmas party right before her untimely death.

Kelly stood on the chair and unpinned the article. She began reading from the beginning. All the while, she had the strangest feeling that the gaze of the young woman in the picture was fixed on her. Wanting her to know what had happened. Mary's story was so tragic.

Killed in a freak avalanche. Suffocated under the weight of the snow.

Staring into her soulful eyes, Kelly wondered what it felt like, alone, buried under all that whiteness.

"Mom said we should watch the Weather Channel." Ryan had hung up the phone and was standing behind her. "What's that?"

"One of Mom's articles. Scary stuff." She pinned it back onto the bulletin board before he could reach for it. "I'm going to my room." She glanced out the window over the sink. The sky remained its usual winter gray. Thick clouds but no storm.

All this craziness over nothing, she thought. *I've been looking forward to this sleepover all week, and now I have to sit here with a babysitter, totally bored.*

She had no idea of the horrors that lay ahead.

WANT MORE CREEPINESS?

Then you're in luck, because P. J. Night has some more scares for you and your friends!

P. J. Night has a secret message for you and your friends to discover at your creepover. Simply use the code to fill in the blanks of the secret message.

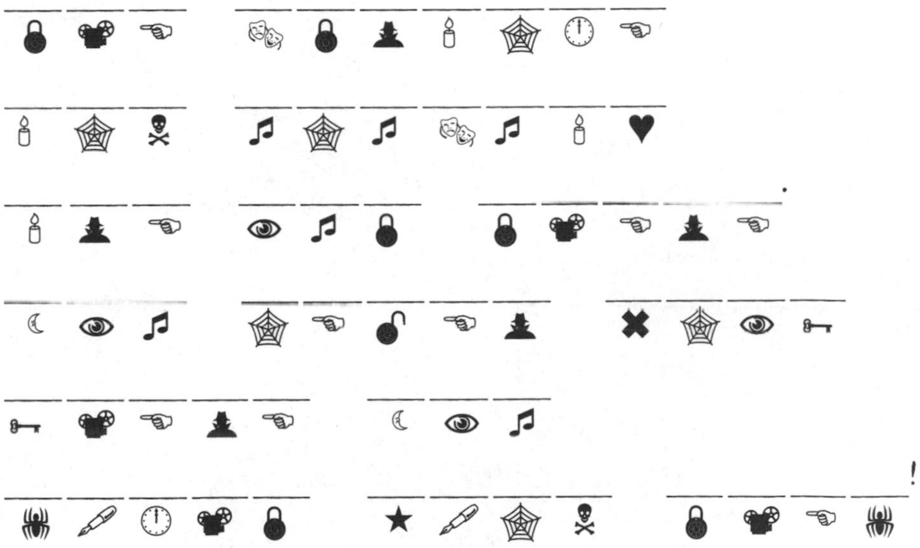

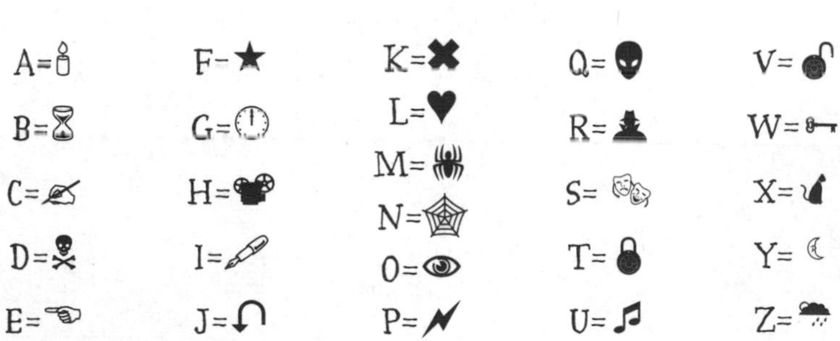

Answer: The strange and unusual are out there. You never know where you might find them!

REPRODUCIBLE

YOU'RE INVITED TO . . .
CREATE YOUR OWN SCARY STORY!

Do you want to turn your sleepover into a creepover? Telling a spooky story is a great way to set the mood. On the next page, P. J. Night has written a few sentences to get you started. Fill in the rest of the story on the lines provided and have fun scaring your friends.

You can also collaborate with your friends on this story by taking turns. Have everyone at your sleepover sit in a circle. Pick one person to start. She will add a sentence or two to the story, cover what she wrote with a piece of paper, leaving only the last word or phrase visible, and then pass the story to the next girl. Once everyone has taken a turn, read the scary story you created together aloud!

(If you don't want to write in your book, use a separate piece of paper.)

When my mom was a little girl, she lived next door to an old, abandoned farmhouse. According to the other kids in the neighborhood, no one had lived there in more than one hundred years. But that didn't mean things didn't happen in there. Every night my mom would see lights turn on and off in different rooms. Her parents didn't believe her, until one night when . . .

_____

_____

_____

_____

_____

_____

_____

_____

_____

_____

_____

REPRODUCIBLE

REPRODUCIBLE

REPRODUCIBLE

REPRODUCIBLE

_____

_____

_____

_____

_____

_____

_____

_____

_____

_____

_____

_____

_____

_____

THE END

REPRODUCIBLE

You're invited to MORE
CREEPOVERS!

HAVE YOU BEEN TO EVERY ONE?

Available at your favorite store!
CREEPOVERBOOKS.com

Looking for another great book?
Find it
IN THE MIDDLE.

Fun, fantastic books for kids
in the in-beTWEEN age.

IntheMiddleBooks.com

 SIMON & SCHUSTER
Children's Publishing   /SimonKids    @SimonKids